STRANGE

STRANGE

STORIES

SHREYA SEN-HANDLEY

HarperCollins *Publishers* India

First published in India by
HarperCollins *Publishers* in 2019
A-75, Sector 57, Noida, Uttar Pradesh 201301, India
www.harpercollins.co.in

2 4 6 8 10 9 7 5 3 1

P-ISBN: 978-93-5357-145-0
E-ISBN: 978-93-5357-146-7

This is a work of fiction and all characters and incidents described in this
book are the product of the author's imagination. Any resemblance to actual
persons, living or dead, is entirely coincidental.

Shreya Sen-Handley asserts the moral right
to be identified as the author of this work.

Typeset in 11/15 Scala at
Manipal Digital Systems, Manipal

Printed and bound at
Thomson Press (India) Ltd

MIX
Paper
FSC FSC® C010615

This book is produced from independently certified FSC® paper to ensure
responsible forest management.

To the Gang of Five, my tale-testers – my husband,
parents and a couple of friends, Kolkata-based NPB
and JJ in B'lore – whose enthusiasm for these stories
helped shape this book

LEAN ON ME

As dawn breaks and I peer at the hundredth hazy picture on yet another police website, I wonder why I'm still doing this, three months on. Then I hear Samrat turning over in his little bed by the window and remember why. We had clung to each other from the day our world had been turned upside down. Since then, Sam has remained in my bedroom though he could have returned to his own. Each night, he falls asleep from sitting up beside me, searching the web for a sign. Any sign that *he* would return, that he might remember, that he had even existed. Why? Because we are hurting still ...

Managing the Restwell Rehab was dreary work that put food on our table. Shrugging on the charcoal-dull custodian coat in the morning while the canteen staff clattered the teaspoons and cups of the breakfast run around me, I would focus on the image of Sam's bed-tousled head and sleepy morning smile to get me through the day. But when Karan joined the shelter, the workday began to hold interest for me, even though going home to Sam was still its high point.

Karan was a wizened thing in a wheelchair, with the face of an embittered orc. I looked after him like I did all the others – competently, meticulously – but my heart wasn't in it, left behind as it was with my little boy every day. As it had been since his father went away. Little Sam had become my world, and I, his (though I did encourage him to forge friendships at school). I, on the other hand, learned to be stoic. A serious, bookish woman, with a certain statuesque charm carefully hidden under many (usually woollen) layers, I was not looking for companionship. Certainly not from my charges. At first, the most I saw or heard of Karan was his high-pitched voice quavering from the shadowy recesses of the common room, registering his protest at some perceived slight or the other. Noted and dealt with, it did not set him apart from the others. When they did wake from their stupor or break out of their make-believe worlds, it was usually to complain. But he, I realised soon enough, was alert. And a little bit more.

I gave him a wide berth till I saw him reading Salinger, a rite-of-passage favourite of mine. All my ward checks were usually conducted in silence but this took me aback enough for me to exclaim, 'Holden Caulfield, I haven't seen you in a while!'

Karan looked up, almost as surprised to find a supposedly sane person addressing Caulfield (or did he imagine my mundane job precluded me from reading?).

For the first time, he cracked a smile in front of me. 'Jane Gallagher, is that really you?'

We didn't stop to draw breath thereafter. It did strike me that my professionalism was being compromised, as I was suddenly talking all day with a patient who came looking for me in the laundry room or kitchen, painfully wheeling himself around, his face contorted in agony. I did try to discourage him but he was determined – 'I don't give up easily.' And I have to admit I grew to depend on his conversation – erudite yet entertaining – to keep me feeling human in the course of the day. His avuncular admiration for my quick mind and strength of character, with a dash of interest in my appearance, felt like a warm, enveloping blanket of validation. It was hard not to enjoy that. It was hard to put him in his place, starved as I was of affection (though I barely admitted that to myself), except for the little-boy love I got from Sam. With time and the exchange of many confidences, it became easy to block out his unfortunate appearance. Easy to grow terribly fond.

He brought poetry back into my life. 'Shall I compare thee to a summer's day?' he would greet me on wet, gloomy mornings, putting a smile on my face. Or more impressively, he would reel off some of his own. Finely honed and lyrical, each was a tribute, he said, to me. I wondered at his amazing ability to perfect those gems overnight. And all for me!

Yet, I experienced a good few hours of hesitation when he asked for my home phone number. It wasn't professional but, more than that, I was intensely protective of the one good thing in my life – Sam – and I let very few newcomers into our world. But it was so good to have someone on the same wavelength to talk to after so long that I succumbed. Soon, we were nattering round the clock. It was important to me that my son was part of my new-found laughter. So I introduced him to Karan, and it wasn't long before my bright boy was enthralled by the latter's yen for yarns and way with the young (as well as with the young-at-heart or, some might say, naïve). They would speak nearly as long on the phone at night as Karan and I.

It was a slow creep (an unfortunate phrase to associate with a disabled man, yet so apt), an insidious taking-over of our lives, till he was not only part of the family but actually in charge. Organising our first Christmas holiday in years for which he was, unsurprisingly, joining us, persuading Sam to spend more time on his clarinet, convincing me to stop losing weight.

'You are already perfect,' he said to me. 'Believe in yourself like I do.' And my heart swelled with gladness. Here was the whole package – a man who was kind, loving and forthright. Appearances can be so deceptive, I thought happily to myself.

Then a letter arrived at Restwell. Unusual in that we don't get such letters but it looked the ticket. It *was* a ticket. It was Karan's Get Out of Gaol pass. Surprisingly, my superior approved it sight unseen, but Karan didn't want to leave. I went from feeling sorry for myself at the prospect of losing him, to happy he would lead a 'normal' life again, to miserable that he had nowhere to go. He had told me about his past over the months we'd been talking and it had reduced me to tears every time. Abused as a child by a violent father who then went on a killing spree, Karan had survived the shooting to spend years in orphanages and recurrently in rehab as an adult, as his deformities, fleeting relationships and short-lived jobs drove him to despair and depression. Consequently, he had neither a home nor a family to go to, or close friends who would welcome him.

On a rainy Thursday afternoon, just before my weekly break, we sat in his quiet corner of the common room, next to the bookshelf he'd made his own. He would go to the homeless shelter on Twelfth Avenue he said, and the soup kitchen down the road would keep body and soul together till he found a job. But how likely was he to find one? Disabled and deeply troubled, he made singularly unfortunate first impressions. I found myself asking him to move in with us, but I struggled with its significance because there was already a whiff of romance about us despite its improbability; a courtly romance of warm, poetic effusions in which I was the muse to his minstrel. Moving in with us, however, would surely precipitate an actual relationship, which I wasn't sure I wanted.

He recited Neruda to me on our rain-ravaged Friday night call.

Snap. Crackle. Pop. Prolonged crackle. And then a bolt, not out of the blue but still sudden. 'I've fallen in love with you,' he said.

The deafening static consuming the line gave me time to think, to quell the panic. I did love him but not in that way. Was it in that way? I didn't know.

'Is something the matter?' He sounded hurt.

'I love you too,' I blurted, and in saying so, it became true.

Saturday morning, he moved in. We lived in a high-rise, so we grappled with makeshift ramps and tiny lifts before safely ensconcing him in the bedroom Sam had given up for him. His presence was not otherwise disruptive because he was so much a part of our lives already. My little boy did seem to spend far too much time fetching and carrying and cleaning up after Karan, which troubled me. But Sam loved him and was happy to help. We had a rosy few months playing happy families, without the sexual complications I'd dreaded, as he would disappear into his bedroom to write poetry every night. But with very little to show me in the mornings, as he once had with such enthusiasm. I felt terrible he wasn't comfortable enough with us to write like he used to.

Despite his ineptitude around the house, he had less trouble getting about the city and he would be gone for large chunks of the day. He said he was looking for work but never found anything suitable, or that he was at the bank, yet the money he expected never arrived. An extra mouth to feed was a strain on my finances in the meantime, but he'd come to mean so much to us, I overlooked it. We were hit with a huge internet bill, which explained the lack of poetry, I thought, but said nothing. He left the tap running in the bath one day, flooding the flat and placing the blame squarely and shockingly on Sam, whom he claimed to love. I confronted him about it and got a gobful in return.

'Stop whining,' he said cuttingly. 'It pushes people away. As you know.'

'How is this about me?' I spluttered when I'd recovered from having the argument turned on me. 'It's you who's been strange. So different from who you are ... were. I just want to understand why.' No explanation was offered, however, and I didn't push further. And life did go back to normal. Almost. He slept in Sam's room, ate our food, but all we had left of his once-charming presence was the disgruntled quavering of his early months at Restwell.

Then one day, I came home early to deal with the landlord's complaint of another leak in my flat. I turned off the overflow in the bathroom and went to find Karan in his room. He wasn't there, which was not unusual, but the flickering, hypnotic computer screen was open on his email account. I found myself drawn to it despite my best intentions. Or maybe my best intentions had deserted me over the last month of doubt and conflict. I was looking for emails to confirm there was money coming in. Instead, I found reams of messages to women. Many women. Spread across the country. As I trawled through them, I discovered they dated back to our good times, when we had been closest and he'd declared his love for me and eagerly moved in.

He had sent each the poetry he claimed he wrote for me. Every single one he hailed as his muse and his only love. 'If irresistible passion, womanly warmth and a razor-sharp intellect wasn't enough, you have the finest pair of eyes that ever graced a face,' he waxed lyrical in one message. I could remember struggling to hide my pleasure when he'd said that to me in the laundry. 'Thank you for coming into my life and making me whole again,' he wrote to another, echoing the words he had said to me one rain-washed afternoon. I could hear the hiss of the rain now. It was the sound of blood rushing to my head. Scouring every last line of those hateful love-filled messages was like the indescribably painful probing of fresh wounds. But I couldn't stop. Not until I could believe what I was reading.

A slight noise behind me made me turn to find him looking at me with unfathomable hatred. I crumbled. Running sobbing from the room, I waited for him to follow, to explain, to soothe, to lie even. But the door clicked shut behind me. Then there was silence. For hours.

I talked through the door, first livid, then coaxing him to speak to me, to explain, in case there was an explanation ... to ease the pain. I banged on the door when he refused to respond, from anger but also fear, in case he did something to himself.

Finally, I gave up and left to get Sam from school. Perhaps we would both calm down and be able to talk it over in the evening. Quietly, so Sam wouldn't twig. He was growing up quickly and sensed unrest.

Sam and I came home to an empty house. Karan had gone. He had taken all his possessions with him. And some of ours.

All except the wheelchair.

LONG IN THE BLUE TOOTH

'Just look at them, no respect for anything. Makes my oil boil!' Robi grumbled, peering at the youngsters swaggering past his little group. They trampled all over the flowerbeds that the retirees themselves tended, cheekily clocking the reaction of the elderly bunch on the porch as they went. They were visitors here and could not be retaliated against. That had been drummed into the Domestics, or Doowies, when they were inducted into this compound after their retirement from household service. And they toed the line, even though the visitors didn't always. There really was a line on the ground neither party was meant to cross during visiting hours, and to make it look more like homes than enclosures, flowers had been planted along them. When the visitors left every evening, the Doowies spruced up their homes and the lines of blossoming shrubbery. And more and more each day they would find that the line had been crossed, the shrubs trampled, the flowers squashed. They felt the transgression in their joints, even when there wasn't physical evidence left behind. The noise the visitors made bothered them too, and none of it in a language comprehensible to them. They were getting on, going deaf, and it all sounded like squawking. None of it was for them anyway. The visitors talked constantly, but into little devices they held. From the depths of what looked like a bundle of laundry left to moulder in an armchair, came the wavering voice of Nawaz, the nonagenarian – 'And what about those things in their ears, Blue Fangs do they call them?' 'Na, na, Shona, Blue Tooth,' said his sprightly eighty-something partner, Pari, who took a more accommodating view of the present. Pari knew Nobs was on to his pet peeve and said nothing further. A good rant before lunch kept Nobs going. And lunch was sure to be a distraction, even though he could only manage a liquid diet these days.

Lunch was as good as it got when they worked in the well-heeled homes of the gated compounds of Gurugram. This was a gated compound too, though farther out, in the wilds of Haryana. And the lunch was fresher, made for them specifically; not leftovers like they were used to having. Of course, that meant it wasn't as fancy, because who made fancy food for a drove of domestic workers? Retired at that. They missed the leftovers from the parties – the succulent kebabs, chi-chi canapés, and posh pastries. Usually distributed to them a good forty-eight hours after, when it was certain that no family members or friends would want them. Still, it was good food. And nothing that a microwave couldn't fix. Micro waves they could do, smartphones were another matter. They had never been allowed any by their employers ('Why would you need to talk to anyone else?'), and even now, watching the youngsters glued to them, they were no wiser. 'What rubbish they seem to be constantly channelling into these things, eh?' Robi said with his permanently superior air. 'Did the stuff said to us back in the day make a lot more sense?' Ketaki recalled. 'Nor did some of the things we were asked to do,' Robi chuckled in remembrance.

'Yes, that! Exactly that!' Ketaki crowed. 'And now we don't have to lift a finger, you see?'

'Yes, but,' Pari tentatively offered, 'I don't know that this is better.'

'We were watched before; we are watched now!' Nobs exploded (but only figuratively; his health was such that he was quite capable of actual self-combustion).

'But,' boomed Ketaki, 'now we don't have to work our rusty assess off! We may not have those thingies those kids keep yapping into, but we are allowed to talk to each other. Finally. We have landed on our creaky feet and ought to be grateful.'

It was true that a decade ago, domestic workers couldn't have hoped to have ended their days this way. Being fed and serviced regularly, with companions through the day, and comfortable beds to retire to at night. Retirement from their jobs in posh homes in the past would have entailed a far more drastic change from what they had become used to. Those well-lit living quarters and well-fed days. They would have headed back to where they'd come from, and ended their days in tiny, darkened back rooms; starving, or surviving on what scraps of menial work came their way from those who looked on them kindly. Not many did. They were the lowest of the low, not human enough; certainly different to look at. And even after all these years of working with 'superior' families, proving themselves well-behaved, even acquitting themselves well in looking after children, they were often still distrusted. Particularly when no longer under the watchful eyes of their employer-families (or Empies). And if they could not be trusted, they were also more likely to be attacked. Especially if they ventured out of the labyrinthine lanes in which their dark little coops resided, in those sprawling Doowie ghettoes most metros now had. Most did not survive the attacks, ending up on the scrapheap. Or that huge out-of-town landfill of shattered limbs and dreams called the Pasture.

Nobs, mulling over all this, had to agree with Kets (as he liked to call her), that this was a far better putting out to pasture, but grumbled nevertheless about the visitors as the lunch bell went, 'And yet, I do not like them scrutinising us in that peculiar way where they seem not to connect to who we are; they look piercingly at us, yet past us, missing our humanity. And the lunch bell is late again.'

'Well, what do you expect from such flim-flam? They are young. They are not robots either,' Robi said smugly. As they contemplated lunch in the long sterile halls, they thanked their lucky stars (or indeed, their starmarks, as the identifying pattern on their ankles were called). This was quite the turn-up for the books. In fact, it may have been dreamt up in a book! Because that's how unreal it sometimes felt to them – this unexpected life, almost luxurious, and yet curiously discomfiting.

Lunch was conducted in silence. Each of them being given a precise amount of food and a fixed amount of time to ingest it. But discipline they were good at, especially of this new lax variety. They also had, if anything, more time for themselves now than ever before. Of course it depended on what you meant by time for yourself – if it was unobserved time then that didn't happen till after shutdown. And there were, sometimes, exclusive programmes that let special groups in at night-time; broadcasters, experts, high-rollers and the like, who wanted to watch other things. Not that there was much to watch at their age, once they'd retired for the night – snoring, drooling and turning over perhaps. And those large greasy patches they left behind every time they turned. It wasn't till they filed out of the long hall to sit in their porches that conversations were struck up again. They were encouraged to talk these days. To smile, to move around (within limits), and be animated. It pleased the visitors. If they spotted the Doowies doing something new, they were more likely to come back. And if something extra exciting went down like the time Uma had massive organ failure, right there on the porch, why, it brought not only regular visitors back in droves, but new ones along with them. And of course, it all happened in the many porticoes of their white clapboard homes (more like cubicles for how small they were inside, but shiny nonetheless), because they weren't allowed back inside till shutdown. Once the day bell had been rung and they were out on their open verandahs, that's where they stayed but for meal breaks. So Nobs, who was winding down, had learned to sleep on the porch itself, sunk in his armchair, oblivious to the shrieking and finger-pointing around him. His armchair was comfier than any other in the compound and that's because he was the oldest Doowie there.

'I cannot believe,' he said, settling into it, 'this is the best they could get. Karma told me in the lunch hall that in that new compound they've built near the India Gate, armchairs are very fancy indeed. Everyone gets one, and for nonagenarians, they are extra, extra special, with backscratchers, cupholders, trays and everything. And look at what I've been lumped with.'

'Come, come, Nobs,' hushed Pari, meaning to calm him by pointing out how comfy his chair was. She had sat in it once and realised how much more comfortable it was than any of their spindly aluminium chairs. But it would only get passed on when he'd wind down altogether, and she didn't even want to think about it. She was interrupted, however, as she usually was, by Ketaki holding forth on the many compounds around the country and what theirs had that those didn't. Pari often wondered if Kets was an Infiltrator Doowie, trained and put amongst them to remind them of their loyalties. Ket amongst the pigeons, she thought to herself and chuckled. But Robi said not, as he had the misfortune of working with her all his life, and she had sung praises of her employers from day one.

The period after lunch always saw more visitors, so Nobs lost himself in a self-imposed stupor to avoid having to cope with their scrutiny. Robi and Ketaki chattered desultorily about old times, while Pari kept an eye on both Nobs, semi-comatose in his chair, and the visitors who seemed more numerous and excitable that particular afternoon. Nobs was woken by high-pitched giggles and screams outside their enclosure. It was Thursday afternoon. Of course. The schools had rolled up for their weekly infotainment about other 'functionals' (the new word for all living things). Even children as young as these were clutching phones in their hands, some had them jammed to their ears, chattering away, or glued to their eyes, when they should've been observing what the teacher was pointing out. The teacher was pointing at them. 'Pointing at us like we're animals!' Robi exclaimed. 'But ask them a question and they're the ones grunting! Barely able to string two words together.'

'And yet,' Nobs suddenly came to life, hoiking himself on to his hobby horse again, 'stick that thing in their ear and they're off, talking nineteen to the dozen. Contraptions more important than human interaction? What's the world coming to?' He shook his head sadly but he was just hitting his stride and enjoying every moment of it. This was the high point of his day. 'Last week,' Dolly, the hitherto silent one said, lighting up and letting rip about the thing that troubled them even more than their situation, 'this odious girl came right up to our enclosure and was mumbling away. I thought she was speaking to me but nooo, she was talking to that weevil in her ear!' 'I know!' Nobs was now properly stirred up. 'I've seen them pouring their poppycock into the things attached to their hands and those in their heads. They talk to friends they are about to meet, friends they've just been with, or those with them at that very minute! Whatever happened to good old-fashioned chinwags?'

'And good manners, and the gracious upbringing that respectable families gave their children?' wondered Robi. 'What gracious upbringing, dear?' Pari interjected finally, 'We lived amongst them, carrying out their orders and trying to keep order, as their children ran riot. After they replaced the servants of their own kind, who were getting uppity they said, they brought us in as domestics and gave us no leeway at all. Their children were allowed to become absolute terrors and kindness died a raucous death.'

'I'm not sure there ever was kindness in the world.' Kets spoke up for the new regime again, but conceded, 'Certainly when they engineered this coup in which their lower classes were substituted in their homes by the likes of us, it became easier for the top echelon to tighten their grip over everything, and teach their next generation to do the same.'

'And here we have it,' sighed Dolly, before slumping back into her habitual silence. They looked glumly out at the sea of schoolchildren that had engulfed their little enclosure. At least it seemed that way. They felt under siege and there was no denying it, even staunchly pro-status-quo Kets was looking nervous. Her bellowed hallooo to the kids had not deterred them in the way she'd hoped. The children continued to manoeuvre closer to the elderly quintet on the porch, as they chattered in their disjointed way on their various handheld and ear-plugged gizmos.

'Well, they talk but not like we do,' Pari offered. She found the new lingo amusing on the whole, but even she was flummoxed when her one young friend in the compound, a carer, had shown her the 'txt' her boyfriend had sent to end their relationship. 'It's far more mechanical. Without the grace of our speech. Squiggles and numbers and letters thrown together haphazardly,' she related to her group now, throwing a worried glance at Nobs, who appeared to be slowly turning a luminescent shade of orange. The sea of younger schoolchildren had parted in the meantime to reveal a more worrying enemy – a group of older schoolkids, more full of themselves, infinitely more clogged up with contempt for those around them. 'It's the devil's own tongue,' Robi agreed, almost matching Nobs in his vehemence, as he indicated the oncoming trio of smirking teenagers with a thin, steely finger. Kets tried to defuse the situation, attempting to turn their minds back to the good lunch they'd had. It had been a special lunch because several functionals from the compound had turned eighty-five. They had had an oily swill, with some mulch, and a watery sweet at the end, instead of their usual bowlful of C-45. It really wasn't bad at all. And ordinarily, this simple trick of turning a functional's mind back to some other event or task had always worked for the Empies. Kets, having risen to housekeeper, had learnt it from the best. But so close were the kids, so overpowering their sounds, gangling limbs, and the smell of their disdain, that even she couldn't keep the quintet's mind off them. 'Now, Nobs, now, you know that's not true. Don't you work yourself up over nothing. They are harmless really, and one day, they will feel as threatened, and as needlessly, by the new generation sweeping in, as we do,' Pari said as calmly as she could, but her panic too was rising, not so much at the children approaching as at Nobs' reaction to it. Her ticker had started racing, and she couldn't begin to imagine what this oppressive situation was doing to Nobs, but she could see from the incandescent fury on his face that the switch had already been thrown, and a fire was raging inside.

Before anyone knew what was happening or how to prevent it, the teens, breaking away from the school group, had jumped over the barrier to mount the porch. 'My god,' whispered Dolly, 'can this really be happening?' In the years since compounds had been established for retired domestic functionals, their enclosures had never been breached. It was unheard of. Despite the indignity of being told what to do every step of the way (which was no different from their working lives), of being herded around and watched every minute of every day, there was one respect accorded to them. They would not be approached by anyone other than the park staff. 'It really is happening,' the unflappable Robi confirmed with a wobble in his voice, even as the first of the teens over the fence, and the most insolent, stuck his face into the former's for a better look. The rest of the school, milling around erratically as they had been, now smelt a fracas and closed in. But for a change, they weren't chattering. It was as if the whole compound held its breath and a little whispered prayer could be heard wafting in the breeze, hoping nothing more untoward happened. It might have been Pari's.

But then, the boy reached out and tore Robi's identifying collar off, pocketing it like a souvenir. A siren went off in the distance almost immediately. Pari saw Nobs move from the corner of her eye and immediately called out to him, 'No, Nobs, no, it'll be fine.' But before she could finish, the second smirking teen had clapped his hand over her mouth and pushed her back into her chair. She fell in awkwardly, crying out as a wave of snide laughter engulfed her. Drawing on every last ounce of his waning nonagenarian energy, Nobs launched himself out of his extra-special armchair and stood up to the youth. He looked diminutive in comparison, but his rage gave him a presence he didn't ordinarily have. 'We have spent our lives looking after you monkeys! And now at the end of our days, can't we be paid a little respect? The humanity you never showed us when we served you? The humanity you refused to credit us with? We were promised that here, that despite being on display, we would never be touched by your grasping, greedy hands again.' The youngsters cackled at this, the most forward amongst them planting his hands firmly on Nobs' frail shoulders and staring him down – 'But you're not one of us, grandpa, you never were! You are waste from the factories that no one could put to any other use. Just rustbuckets!' If there was a grain of truth in it, Nobs was beyond reason now. Somewhere in the background, he heard another one of the little monsters say, 'Only scrap. Little better than shit. We did you a favour.' He also picked up on Pari still trying, despite her own shock and alarm, to defuse the situation. 'Nobs,' he heard her murmur again and again. Her voice in his head spurred him on to the final gallant thing he would ever do. His voice crackling with the last of his energy, he yelled, 'Take it then, you fools. Take back what belongs to you!' With that, he tore out his arm and threw it at them, hitting one squarely on the forehead, leaving a deep steel burn, and grazing the other. The sparks flying from the exposed wires in the open socket of the flying arm showered down on the children who had pushed closer and closer as the fight developed, scattering them.

The biggest boy to have breached the enclosure, now sporting a brand much like the Doowies, had a look of intense malevolence on his face. Grabbing hold of what remained of Nobs, he threw him onto the wooden floor of the porch with a resounding crash. He was about to grind him down with his foot, when the compound manager came hurtling through the crowd, the siren triggered minutes ago having brought him to the heart of the trouble. 'Break it up, break it up!' he rushed in screaming, but then he saw the mangled functional at his feet and came to a shocked stop. The orderlies who had come tearing in behind him escorted the children off, but with the kid gloves required by the all-powerful Empies. Shaq, the compound manager, gingerly touched the side of Nobs' face, where a beating valve existed to monitor the energy left in a Doowie. Robi muttered to himself, unlikely to ever recover his equanimity, even as the ever-buoyant Kets gave in to her tears.

Only Pari did not make a noise. When the unit manager shook his head and got off his haunches, Pari approached him emotionlessly, and offered him her arm. 'You are sure?' asked Shaq, deeply unhappy with the brouhaha at the compound on what was usually their best day of the week, but most of all with this latest development. At Pari's nod, he took her arm and deftly flicked the switch on the wrist. She crumpled to the floor next to Nobs, jolting to a final halt, but not before every tarnished joint and aged lever had groaned a last protest. Rounding on the remaining trio, the unit manager grumbled, even as he felt sorry for what they'd been through that day, 'We could've slung you out to Pasture as we used to. But we took you in, kept you ticking. Gave you a better twilight. Nothing is perfect after all. Maybe you should learn to appreciate what you have.' But they were lost somewhere in the ether now, back in the Coldrooms in which they'd been born. They were certainly not listening any more. He walked away with a sigh, leaving a carer to steer the Doowies back into their daily routine, if it could be done at all with those three. He had a bad hunch he'd be several Domestics down soon, and it would be a while before he could replace them. Robot domestics were becoming rarer and rarer, he thought wistfully, as other more docile functionals were being created to take their place.

As night fell on the Gurugram Robots' Retirement Park, and the shutdown forced visitors home, more excited than he'd ever seen them – their fingers flying over tiny keypads, little smartphone cameras flashing, and a few talking intently into those invisible pods in their ears; the Blue Teeth that had so troubled Nobs only hours before – the park manager wondered if life could ever go back to how it used to be.

THE PROBLEM WITH POTATOES

They stared at her, open-mouthed, when she walked in, leaving Sumi to wonder why. After all, *they'd* asked her over. At her first proper job interview on graduating from her all-girls college in Calcutta, and teetering on the verge of a less sheltered life, she felt as exposed as an uncooked potato waiting to be dropped in oil. She fervently hoped they couldn't catch it in the nervous wobble in her voice, only to realise they were more interested in her appearance. She had got a lot of that recently, especially since she had arrived in Delhi. The only woman on the interview panel eventually smiled, almost sympathetically, and opening the portfolio of bylines for big Calcutta dailies the girl had left earlier, said, 'You write beautifully; would you like to be a trainee, here?' At which the men harrumphed nervously, till she added, 'It would be a behind-the-camera position though, if you're happy with that.'

The stipend offered was tiny, yet the job was perfect for her in every other way, so, naturally, she took it. But she had no idea where to stay and worse, she didn't know how to break the news to her anxious parents that she wasn't coming home. 'Where will you live? *How* will you live?' her mother sounded shocked, but not, fortunately, tearful. 'It seems too soon. Are you ready for it?' This irritated Sumi. *Of course she'd be fine.* She was young, but of age. And she hadn't used up all her lives yet. Her mother said, ever after, that at this moment, her hair turned grey. But if she were honest, she would have to admit the greying had preceded her daughter's bid for freedom by a decade.

Finding a place to rent in the city proved far more difficult than getting a job. Single, young and conspicuous, she scoured Delhi for a suitable place to stay. The choices were varied in that each was more horrific than the last; from a warren of hutches for a horde of perpetually stoned women to rooms that reeked of something sinister that was neither smell nor atmosphere, but the fact that the only way in or out, was through the leering landlord's bedroom.

She rejected these for a place owned by the most massive woman she'd ever met. It had felt relatively safe, yet the claustrophobia engendered by tiny windows, rigid house rules and an ever-watchful male servant, soon found her homeless again. With the arrest of a roommate for public obscenity (a.k.a. necking with a boyfriend in the back of a car parked in a dark alley) and the resultant gossip amongst Delhi-based familiars of a certain age about Sumi's own 'wild and wanton' life (if only, she thought), she finally gave up searching for a place of her own.

By then, her problems with accommodation – though not rare in that city, but made infinitely more interesting because of her way with words – had spread all over the office. People nodded in sympathy as she walked past; some came up with alternatives, which reconnoitres revealed to be as revolting as the ones she'd rejected. A few friends put her up from time to time in university dorms, shared dives, or impossibly small barsatis where the single bed would be occupied in turn. This handful of large-hearted friends ran the risk of expulsion for 'subletting' (though no transactions in cash or kind took place). Their kindness warmed her even more than the occasional roof over her head. Intermittently, someone senior and prosperous would take her home to feed and she'd crash on their sofa – that was as far as it went. A good thing, she thought, mostly. Sometimes, there was a whiff or even the pong of other intentions, but those advances were not from the more desirable men; it was the lonely, gauche, far-from-home younger ones that made them. They did not tempt her with their clumsy interest. She chose, on nights when she had no other option, to stay within the safe confines of the basement television studio in South Delhi where she worked. Sumi learned to bat away mosquitoes and hunger with equal élan after the first few months.

One night, she wandered into the gloom of a late edit. It was a cold night and she had wrapped a scarf round her face and head. Inside the room, she could see the dim outline of the most interesting man in her office – Rahul. He was handsome in a tall, dark, craggy way. He had bags of confidence and a rather brusque, teasing way with women that they lapped up. She didn't mind a bit of it herself, but it didn't come her way much. As she approached the huddled form on the chair and squeaked hello, he whipped around and jumped. In the interminable pregnant pause, he collected himself in what seemed like slow motion, reached out and tugged at her scarf. She was acutely aware of his fingers brushing her cheek. She wondered whether she was meant to scold or step away. Try, as she might, the sense of such rules eluded her. She liked how it felt, so she stayed put. But then, he wrapped the scarf back round her face like a burkha, and said, 'Your eyes have such fire in them. I want to look at those alone.' He then gave her the slightest shove towards the door, so gentle you couldn't complain, but as she stumbled back out into the common room to try and snatch some sleep that night, she couldn't help the hurt that swamped her.

Later, huddled on a sofa, she touched her face gingerly, wondering if anyone would ever look past it again. The feel of her cold, ruched skin brought back memories of another day; the kind of day that insidiously sneaks into dreams even as it is wilfully forgotten in the waking hours.

Sure enough, she dreamt she was back in the half-light of that Calcutta dawn. In her excitement at being off to the airport to nab cricketing hero, Steve Waugh, for an interview, she hadn't given much thought to the driver of the hired car the paper had sent. But when his head lurched forward the first time, Sumi felt her exhilaration turn to a cold anxiety. Was the man falling asleep? She started talking to him. Loudly, to keep him awake. He looked at her dismissively in the rear-view mirror as if he couldn't be bothered to answer someone so young and female. His bloodshot eyes worried her even more. Was he also drunk? 'Stop,' she said, and again. But the car kept going. And the next time she met his eyes in the mirror, the unsteady, resentful stranger had morphed into Rahul. She awoke, feeling frazzled.

Thereafter, quite unwillingly, she developed a Rahul-radar, knowing instantly when he was in the room by the prickling of her hair. She would make a big show of not looking at him when really she was sneaking glances, all the while. She heard his laughter at office parties, followed by the answering tinkle of a female giggle and felt a twinge, no, a deep stab of jealousy. But he wasn't even aware she existed. Or if he was, he didn't care. He never looked at her or said hello, much less try and touch her again. She, on the other hand, had a massive, hopeless, yawning chasm-like crush that was taking up too much headspace. She reapplied herself to her work, but somewhere at the back of her mind, or like a tiny splinter in her heart, was the memory of how she felt about him, just waiting to be rekindled.

That feeling reawakened one winter evening, when she was looking for a place to spend the night. No suitable digs had presented themselves for months, and tonight, the office was being pest-controlled. All the office vermin were at risk, including her. But she had found none of her usual saviours, despite a whole morning spent searching for them in the nooks and crannies of their basement office. The common room, too, appeared deserted when she settled down to handwrite an outline for her next story. Scratch, scratch, scratch, went her pen. Screech, replied a chair. Pulled forward into the light from the dark corner in which its inhabitant had been dozing after a night edit. Rahul leaned forward and said, so softly she almost didn't hear, 'Do you have somewhere to spend the night?' They were his first words to her since their night-time collision in the edit suite and only the second time he had spoken to her. 'No,' she said hesitantly, not at all sure where it was leading, not at all wanting to seem in need of his help. 'Come back with me,' he commanded, in no doubt that someone in need of a bed would want his; especially his. 'Gopal will make you luchi aloo dum in the morning.'

This confused her. Was he proposing breakfast for her services or was it a straightforward offer, from the kindness of his heart, of a bed for the night and breakfast in the morning? That she didn't have a place to stay was common knowledge, but he'd never cared before. And it wasn't his large heart he was known for. But she still felt a little puff of warmth forming inside, expanding as she thought of his kindness into a cloud of good feeling. Then, that other thought struck her again, and the cloud popped. He was a notorious womaniser, and even though she was the farthest thing from his type, it clearly didn't matter on a slow-woman day. She would be nothing more than a notch on his bedpost, when she wanted to be much more. Yet, she felt a tingling anticipation, a head-swimming excitement beginning to mount. She said yes and proceeded to worry about it all day.

He came looking for her late in the evening, just as she was contemplating dredging up another acquaintance with a spare bed for the night. He led her to an old Volkswagen, parked carelessly on the studio's dusty drive. If the wayward parking screamed 'I'm too cool for school', the car itself was attention-grabbing in that painstakingly planned contrarian manner of his; a rust bucket of a rare model in a sombre colour, to shore up his intellectual pretensions. But that's what she thought later. At that moment, heading for what lay in wait at his home, she was too besotted and too nervous to care about anything other than being with him in the enfolding, forgiving darkness.

Climbing the dimly lit stairs of Rahul's apartment building in the 'nice' neighbourhood of Chittaranjan Park, she remembered the weeks she'd spent in a rented room nearby, with a door leading to the landlord's lodgings that only locked on his side. She hadn't slept a wink till a friend helped her move the heavy wooden wardrobe in front of the disturbing door. The landlord had found her in contravention of her contract for moving furniture without his permission and she was out on the street again. The memory almost made her turn tail and run, but then she thought – what's the worst that could happen?

Rahul wasn't an axe murderer. Every woman he dallied with turned up to work the next morning. At best, it would be a comfy, mosquito-free bed for the night, and at worst, an exciting experience with a man she was drawn to. Or maybe that would be the best bit.

He shut the door behind her and walked down the corridor. But she hung about the door, shifting her waifish weight from foot to foot. She expected 'Gopal' to emerge from the gloom. To offer them dinner. She thought Rahul would sit her down in the living room like any host with a new guest; they'd have a chat and a cuppa. Or maybe Scotch which she knew he liked (the girls at work talked about him incessantly). She would have declined and asked for a gin and tonic instead. She liked fruity drinks. Would he think her a child?

It was dawning on her that he didn't think of her as a child or a guest. He was holding a door open. Even from the other end of the corridor, she could see the very large bed within. Fear and mortification engulfed her as she walked towards the room in slow motion. Marooned, standing between the door and the bed, she searched Rahul's face for some emotion. Whatever his intention, a smile, a softening of his expression, would have calmed her nerves, but he was poker-faced. As he gestured towards the bed, she sat on it with an anxious thump. He scanned the room as if he were setting up a television shoot. 'Take your top off,' he said gruffly, as he moved a desk lamp nearer so she sat in a pool of light. With no illusions left about his intentions, she ran through the options very quickly in her head: a) she could have heartless, humiliating sex, b) she could bolt, or c) she could talk him into letting her stay the night, minus the shenanigans. As she cleared her throat to suggest Plan C, he exasperatedly ripped her shirt off. In one swift, practiced movement. As she watched buttons clattering into the corners of the room, he proceeded to unclasp her bra in a manner so vexed and disinterested, she could have been a particularly recalcitrant piece of meat he was carving for dinner. Her legs felt heavy, her throat had gone dry, so she squeezed her eyes shut, hoping in her inexperienced way that it would make it go away. Instead, her eyelids burned as an orange glare pierced them. She opened her eyes to see the desk lamp pointed at her in Abu Ghraib fashion. Then, he slapped the lamp's neck down impatiently, so it focused on her breasts. 'I don't need to see the rest,' he growled. She gasped. And then, something began to burn inside her. It was not desire.

She felt like a snake's intended prey, snagged in its hypnotic gaze, knowing death to be imminent but unable to move. And it *was* a snake staring at her, not just the snake in the grass he had turned out to be, but his trouser snake, out now, in his cupped hand, looking at her with its sly beady eye, making her stomach churn. She was terrified he would try to make her touch the thing, or worse, put it in her mouth. Instead, he began to stroke it himself. She was irrelevant in this equation; it was between him, his penis and that lamp he had trained on her breasts. The last so important, he stopped fondling himself for a minute to ensure its light stayed squarely on her nakedness. He was close to doing The Nasty now. But just as he leaned in for the spill, she rolled away. No longer in awe of him, Sumi knew she didn't want his repugnant spunk on her. Screaming 'Bitch!' in frustration, he came all over the bedspread and himself. Then, he stormed out like a diva whose waterbed had deflated. The sound of the front door slamming meant he wouldn't be back for a while. For the night, she hoped, as she carefully locked the door and stripping the bed, lay down to sleep. It was 1 am. She knew from experience, running out into the Delhi night would not be wise. The pervert's bedroom had become the safest place in the city. She slept. And she dreamt.

She was back in the car taking her to Calcutta airport. It weaved erratically as she yelled at the driver, slouched unnaturally over the steering wheel. 'What ARE you doing? Are you awake? Are you unwell? Can you hear me?' And then rolling down the window, 'Can anyone hear me? Help, someone, please!' Her frantic shrieks were sucked into the maelstrom of screaming metal speeding past on one of Calcutta's busiest roads, even at that time of the day. She watched horrified as the driver's head smashed into the steering wheel with a resounding thwack and the car careened out of control. Then, something large and heavy ploughed into them.

She awoke in a strange room with a bitter taste in her mouth and found she'd chewed her lip raw in her sleep. There was blood on the pillow. Spunk on the sheets on the floor. She remembered where she was, and opened the bedroom door a chink to observe the lay of the land. Sunshine had flooded the mise-en-scene. A man was singing in high-pitched, rustic Bengali. Not Rahul. Gopal, perhaps? Wrapping her gap-fronted top around her, she inched out to assess him. Perps sometimes work in pairs after all. But Gopal was the opposite of his employer. Small, unprepossessing and to her relief, smiling.

'Uthechhen?' he beamed. 'Bekphasht baniyechhi.'

Had he known she was there all along, or was he just used to seeing strange women in the morning? She wondered about post-molestation etiquette; should she or shouldn't she stay for breakfast? She decided that food (she hadn't had any since lunch the previous day) might settle her somersaulting stomach. Peeking inside the silver tureens, she was unable to hide her disappointment at the absence of the promised aloo dum. There was luchi though, with an aromatic cauliflower in cumin accompaniment. Gopal saw her face fall and said apologetically, 'Aloor dosh achhe.' She dropped the ladle with a clatter. Was this an admission of Rahul's peccadilloes?

'Hya, aloor dosh acche,' he said again, sadly, 'tai aloo dum banate parlam na, Mish. Dukkho korona, arek din eshe aloo kheo.' I bloody won't, she thought, not any kind of aloo Rahul had to offer, but smiled sweetly – it wasn't Gopal's fault his employer was a jerk, and the phoolkopi he was now spooning up for her smelled delicious. 'E barir kechkola ta-o dekhe joto ta bhalo hobe mone hoye, kokhonoi hoi na,' he gave her a snaggle-toothed grin. She was sure now he was referring to his employer.

She tittered, then guffawed, and Gopal joined her. She felt so much better for it, almost as if the humiliation of last night hadn't happened. Like all she was doing was having a hearty breakfast cooked by this sweet old man who was also taking the trouble to make her laugh. She decided she could laugh the whole incident off. Till Gopal put a folded currency note down beside her. Five hundred rupees. 'Shaart chhire gechhe bole,' he said, as if it had been an accident. Worse, they thought she could be bought, and for such a paltry sum! Whilst she couldn't make up her mind which part of this offended her most, she was relieved that no services had been rendered, he had done it all himself.

She walked out. Then, she ran, putting as much distance as she could between herself and the seeping horror of the previous night, as if it had only just hit her. Hit her with the force of the two-ton lorry that had railroaded her car that fateful day. It may have been months ago, but she still remembered that ear-shattering screech, then being thrown in a blur of twisting metal and flailing limbs, that ended with overwhelming pain. Agony like she'd never known before. But her face felt ice-cold. Strangely, considering she had been in the back seat, her cheek was resting against the windshield. Resting was the wrong word, pinned was more like it – with shards of glass she could see from the corner of her eye. It should have been excruciating but the pain was already receding. Darkness rushed in to take its place.

When she came to, people had gathered around her. There was no shattered glass. No blood or unbearable pain. No twisted, pulverised metal. She was lying on the road, but a narrow, pungent side road – a gali. She wasn't in the midst of the carnage of half a year ago. She was in the present, minutes from Rahul's South Delhi apartment. Did she fall, she asked the people propping her up. Just like that, they told her, nothing had struck her.

'You are fine, Beti, thank god,' said the kindly old lady peering at her. 'So what is that on your face?' 'My face?' Sumi wondered, woozily. Then, she knew. It was so much a part of her now; she sometimes forgot it was there. But not for long. Because nobody else did.

She pulled the little mirror out of her handbag. It was tiny and she could only see half her face in it. She moved the mirror slightly so she could see the other half. The half she usually avoided looking at. That half everyone else averted their gaze from. The half Rahul had blocked out on each of their encounters. She scrutinised the mashed up half, the disfiguring, crinkled scar that gave her face the look of a partially blighted potato. Another aloo with a dosh.

She would have to live with the legacy of her terrible accident, her pulped aloo face, but why should she, or any woman, put up with Rahul's dosh? She now knew what she had to do. And as she headed for her office, with knees scuffed from the fall, top torn from the previous night's humiliation and face shredded from the crash of

six months ago, she could hold her head high. She was
sure she was just one in a long line of mistreated women.
All the heated talk about Rahul was from the women who
were waiting to be chosen. Never from those who had had
the privilege. Well, she would change that.

She didn't have to worry about losing face after all.

THE BONE OF CONTENTION

'Oooh, look at what ol' Sarge has brought in!'

The kids were terribly excited. Huddling around stringy old Sarge and his discovery, they discussed the find excitedly. 'It's a whale bone,' the middle one insisted, but the eldest knew better – 'No, it's too short. Whale bones are long and curvy. Remember the whale skeleton at the museum?' 'Gosh, it took up the entire ceiling!' 'And it dripped,' the littlest one piped up. 'It did NOT drip,' the eldest could be heard sneering as the conversation made its way to some other part of the labyrinthine house.

Sarge was delighted. This was the most attention he'd got in years, and he resolved to find more bones for his new people. He knew just where to go, too. Somewhere he hadn't been allowed in a long while. But there was a new spring in his hobbled old steps, which made everything possible again. He hadn't known what to think when this swarm of children had taken over the grand old house, but now he felt it was for the best. They made a lot of noise. Like Sarj with Sarge. They grabbed at things, including Sarge himself. Sarge was no longer used to being grabbed and cuddled. Not since Sarj had gone away. Sarge didn't mind the affection at all, somewhat overwhelming though it was, especially for a mangy old dog that had hardly been touched in over a decade. Though he wasn't willing to part with the bones he had begun digging up. Oh no, these bones were his. He wouldn't even chew on them. Nor play with them. Certainly not let tiny hands maul them. Not these bones. He knew better than anyone they were special.

The long shank he had brought in today, for example, after a couple of days of bringing smaller fragments in and not minding too much while the children pored over his treasures, he had kept to himself. Guarded it, even bared his teeth at the children once, watching them promptly scuttle away. They didn't know Sarge well enough to realise he was all bark and no bite. 'Woah, what teeth!' said the eldest, trying to hide her alarm. 'Yellow and long and curvy,' squealed the middle one, 'just like those whale bones!' 'NOT going to get bitten!' The youngest one picked up his heels and ran, with the eldest muttering as she followed, 'You and your whale bones.' When they'd gone, Sarge hugged it to himself, almost melding with it. Only letting the children's father have a look at it later (though Sarge, old mutt that he was, had trouble thinking of the young man he'd known at a much younger age as anybody's father). But he had as much right, Sarge decided, to touch that bone as he did. It was close to the bone for him too, so to speak (or bark).

That night, Sarge dreamt; whimpering in his sleep, with his legs vigorously treading air. He was back on the smooth, green lawns of the big house, sprinting in the sun. Running alongside 'his human', Sarj. Sarj had long legs like Sarge, who was a big, shaggy hound. The latter was glossy and muscular back then though, also like Sarj, and not the least bit like he looked now; unkempt and creaky. That humans and their dogs are often alike is no lie, Sarge thought. Sometimes, they even shared a soul, he sighed. Of course, Sarge had grasped that early. Sarj, on the other hand, was a happy, frolicking sort, who really didn't look into anything too deeply. Managing, as a result, to name Sarge an incongruous 'Fluff' (or something, the old dog muttered darkly to himself, seventeen years on). Sarge was no Fluff and would just not respond, till one day, someone called him Sarge and he never answered to anything else again. This created a strange situation. Because of course, Sarj and Sarge sounded the same, and Sarj was resistant at first. But over time, even Sarj liked the silliness of calling his dog by his own name. And of course, humans who could spell (some, slightly more than dogs), could tell the difference. Sarj was the shortened form of a Punjabi name, Sarabjit. Sarge, however, was quite fittingly an army name for a rangy, regal dog.

He would never look like that again, thought Sarge, half-dreaming still, but he had regained the bounce in his gait (as much as his arthritis-riddled shambling paws would allow) since the children had returned. And their father, once as beloved of Sarge as Sarj. They had moved to Australia to make a life away from the gloom of the old hall, but were back at their Grandma's request. And things were afoot. That renewed spring in Sarge's step was not restricted to him alone. It could be seen through the house. A springtime of the spirit was blossoming after long years of winter in the house which had forgotten how to laugh or love extravagantly. This house that had been slowly segregated till parts of it were no longer ventured into. One such part was the cottage with its own little patch at the bottom of the garden. That had been physically fenced off. The original boundary, more like an English hedgerow, had sheltered the vegetables that grew within, but now, the fence was there to ensure nothing at all grew; not even pockets of sunshine. There hadn't been anyone there in years either, allowing the weeds to take over totally. And the exuberance that had been the hallmark of the cottage at the end of the garden, had receded and receded till it had left the whole estate behind, escaping to the hills around it.

Not just the cottage, but the long winding corridor that led to the farthest wing of the house had been sectioned off and become shrouded in shadow. This is where Sundeep now spent his days. If Sarj was sunshine and Sarge was wisdom (strange though that role reversal was), then Sundeep was the Shadow Man. Sundeep himself couldn't shake this feeling off, so never mind other people. He always seemed to be in someone's shadow. First, it was his uncle, monarch of all he surveyed – the tea estates around them, the big house and long lawn, the cluster of shops and workshops at the bottom of the hill. *And* the cottage at the end of the garden. It all belonged to his bachelor uncle, till one day, in a shocking abandonment of familial duty, he snubbed his only brother's only son by bequeathing half his property to a friend's boy. It was as if he didn't care how things were meant to be done. As if he didn't care for Sundeep himself. Sundeep was shocked, and had argued with the old man about the lack of wisdom behind his extravagant, unseemly giving-away of the thing that mattered most to their family – the grand old house. It was as if he had descended precipitately into the chaos of senility. 'Do you see the damage you will do to generations of us? Snatching the ground from beneath our feet? And beyond the trauma and impoverishment, how does it make you look, Uncle? Mean, and, quite possibly, unstable.' It had not endeared him to his uncle but it had wrung out the assurance that the house was his to stay in for as long as he wanted. It's true that Sarj had always lived there too, having been orphaned at an early age and left with his father's best friend. It was also true that the old man left the business to Sundeep alone, recognising Sarj's lack of business sense. 'Or any sense,' Sundeep muttered to himself. But the house, the beautiful house, their family's home for hundreds of years, was left to this stranger from another flock! Sarj may have grown up in that house, but he had always been more pet than son. And when the old man went, leaving his beloved house to the interloper,

Sundeep felt forced into the ignominy of dwelling in Sarj's long, lean shadow. Sundeep brooded over this often, even fifteen years after Sarj had left everything behind to disappear into the blue, as was his wont.

'Irresponsible,' Sundeep now shuddered. Which is what he'd told everyone else as well at the time, completely persuaded of it himself. In the murky light of his sick room, he counted on his withered fingers the many other things that Sarj had done that were feckless. Sinking into that old resentment, he was suddenly prodded into a rare upright position by a noise outside his door. His wife got up from her window seat, where she was a fixture with her book, to plump up his pillow and settle down. 'There's no one outside, don't worry.' She had seen the children wandering the gardens after all.

But there *was* someone outside. It was Sarge. He had walked the entire length of the gloomy corridor he rarely ventured into, to stand outside the door of the Shadow Man. He hadn't done it in a while, but things had changed in the last few weeks. Vitality had revisited him along with the children, who egged him on to get out and about once more. And he had, finding himself at the cottage after fifteen human years, as a result. While exploring that site of so much happiness, something inexplicably tugged at his heartstrings and then pulled, positively pulled on his nose, leading him to a mound in the shade of its eaves. He had dug because the weight of his decade and a half of doggie instincts had instructed him to dig. And digging and digging, he had struck gold. Doggie gold, at any rate.

He had found bones. Long bones, stubby bones, muddy bones and fragments of bone. They had been there a while clearly, picked clean of flesh by the elements. He had felt immediately possessive about the bones. Such a haul would turn any dog's head but this one felt special. He had first taken one back to his manky basket in the corner of the cavernous old kitchen. When that had gone unnoticed, Sarge had brought back more, and the children, always swarming around him, had spotted and scrutinised them. And then this last time, of course, he had managed to bring back a long shank the children had declared a whale bone. Sarge knew, in his bones, that it wasn't. And he knew the man who could tell him more. He found himself hobbling down the length of the corridor that ran along the top floor soon after.

'Who is that?' Sundeep quavered.

Inside the hushed room, with a look of alarm on his deeply grooved face, he started mumbling to himself, 'It's you, isn't it? I knew you'd come for me. But I have something I need to do first.' The nurse ran out to call his wife. Leela, of course, was never far, having shrunken into herself, too, over the years. He looked at her with relief as she entered, and his fingers stopped working at the bed sheet. That whole-bodied trot he'd heard had been a signal. A sign that his tenure was over as he knew it would be one day. That he hadn't long to wrap it up before life was restored to how it used to be. Messy, inappropriate and *wrong*. 'We need to talk,' he said to her, which amused Leela. How often had she said that and been batted aside (figuratively; his general grouchiness never ever flared into a temper)? Outside the room, light footsteps sounded again. 'There', he said in an agitation, 'there it is again. He's back.' 'Young Rav is back, yes, with his family in tow. You wanted it, too. To settle them into the house you would leave to them, while you were still around. Now that they're back, you mustn't forget how young these children are. And kids make noise. They know no barriers. It is their house now anyway, and we don't want to restrict their wanderings in it, do we?' He nodded in agreement distractedly, but with the curtains having been pulled aside to let sunshine wash over the sickroom, he, too, knew it couldn't be them.

Sarge had, in the meantime, shambled back to his dark corner in the kitchen. He had trotted right up to the door of his long-time friend and foe's bedroom. He'd even nudged it gently, half-deciding that it was time. Then something had warned him it wasn't yet, and he had withdrawn, leaving that encounter for another day. He was more persistent with the bones though. Every morning he would race out as fast as his old legs would carry. On the mound he had found in the cottage patch, he would work away busily as if on a mission of great import. As if dogs could have purpose! Although, in the old days, Sarge had always strutted about like the mini-regimental that he was, while Sarj had lounged about languidly. Now, the dog dug like his life depended on it. Or his death. He dug up strangely shaped bones this time. Bones that could not have belonged to anything he himself had buried in this garden in the gilded past when he'd played there regularly. While Sarj would've loitered and looked around him at the abundance of happiness in his life and smiled, which is the kind of thing he did. Sarge, however, had a keener understanding of the gravity of things. And he was appalled when he found the hand.

At the big house, the reaction to this one was different. The children still pored over it, speculating on which wizard might have lost it in a magical duel. 'Newt, surely, Newt,' said the middle sprog. 'It wouldn't be Newt, would it, Silly?' laughed the all-knowing eldest, 'It'd be Gellert Grindelwald. Only a wizard who overreached himself could lose a hand.' The adults, on the other hand, went into a bit of a flap for the first time. It was the most obvious human fragment yet. There was a flurry of huddled conversations. Even the old lady emerged from the darkened wing to be consulted. The cook, the cleaner, everyone, had a look at the cluster of bones, though all hesitated to touch it, unlike the children. Till the latter were sharply reprimanded for it and sent on their way. Then, the police were called. The one rotund constable in charge of the estate police station rolled up the hill to see them. 'What have we here?' he said in his jovial way. That was before he saw the hand. Once he'd seen that, his brows furrowed and he wanted to see what else Sarge had brought in. His entire collection was turned out of its hiding place and inspected. Sarge was then urged to lead the way to his mound of treasured bones in the patch beside the summer cottage.

Every last bone was dug out, even as Sarge mourned the chance to do it himself. His mornings would have less meaning now, he knew. There wouldn't be the same urgency to race to the cottage patch, to spend time with what he loved best. Huffing and puffing, the constable and his minions dug to the bottom of the trough, unearthing an entire skeleton in the process. And in the end, the fat little man with hardly any drama in his life held aloft a skull, as if he'd made a great discovery. A skull with a hole in it. I'm the one who'd made this great discovery, Sarge thought, sinking into himself again, now that his adventure was over. He had discovered the mound and its contents; the constable had only come in for the applause at the end.

The almost-intact skeleton was then carted off to the city, the constable told them in the drawing room, as the sun set on a day of unprecedented upheavals on the estate that had only known peace since the turbulent days of the freedom movement. Oh, there was that small matter of Sarj disappearing, which had caused a brief to-do, but that had all been handled by Sundeep with his customary cool. What ripples it had left behind were emotional. In every other way, the estate had carried on as usual in Sundeep's capable hands. Only in the house that Sarj had inherited and lived in since he was orphaned, was there consternation. The staff had taken a benign interest in the sunny young man from the day he became a part of the house, the women on the estate had evinced a keener interest as he grew, but no one had loved him quite as much as his dog. Spending every waking moment with him, attuned completely to his distinctively sleepy rhythm, Sarge loved him more than life itself. And so, when Sarj disappeared, so did the Sarge everyone knew.

Then, there were fifteen years of quiet but glum efficiency. Till today, with all its turmoil. News reached the old man in his perpetually dusky corner too. 'Are they coming for me, Leela?' 'Who?' she asked, without a ripple on her serene face. 'The police,' he muttered darkly, 'I saw them on the grounds.' 'They were looking for me.' 'No,' she said reassuringly, 'no, they weren't looking for you at all. Why would they? They found something in the cottage garden.' 'Nothing that need upset you,' she coaxed, though she knew better. He said nothing more that night. He was not just thinking hard, he seemed to have receded into some space in his head, a memory perhaps from long ago. In the morning, when Leela came in with the frugal breakfast of oats his illness allowed him, he stated softly, 'I know what they found in the garden.' She pretended not to hear him; she didn't feel ready for the revelation she knew had been coming for the last few years. Maybe even fifteen years. 'I have something to tell you,' he rasped, more insistently than anything he'd said in a while. He sat up, ready to tell her the story she was sure she didn't want to hear. He was at the end of his life now. Why not leave their memories undisturbed?

Leela wanted nothing to do with any of it – house, estate, and the mysteries that swirled around them. She had never desired any part of it, much less have it

become the very centre of their existence, like Sundeep
had. She would leave it all behind once he'd gone. Which
was imminent, and she was quite frankly relieved. She
felt a loyalty to him, of course, that would ensure she
protected him to the end, but shielding was so much
easier if you didn't know what was lurking beneath. And
what horrific discovery now skulked in that cottage she'd
meant to move to when it was all over, she didn't want
to know. It was for her it had been re-opened and was
being renovated. What have I done, Leela, in her dismay,
almost said aloud.

An unfamiliar, less reverent knock on the door
interrupted her thoughts. It was a policeman, she saw to
her alarm, and not the one she knew. And just behind, in
the shadows, she was sure she saw old Sarge hovering, but
when she called out to him, he melted away with an ease
he hadn't shown in years. Just for a moment, she thought
she saw Sarj too. But the policeman marching in with the
pigeon-chested importance of all officialdom demanded
her attention. In a stentorian voice, the unknown
policemen made an announcement. 'In the garden by
the cottage, at the bottom of the estate ...' he began slowly
and deliberately, even as Leela itched to eject him from
the room, and the local constable lurking behind him,
looked uncomfortable and apologetic. 'We have found a
skeleton,' he continued, drawing it out portentously as if
announcing a special guest, 'and it is that of a human.' He
looked around, satisfied that he had dropped a bombshell,
except that his colleague already knew. While Leela,

steeling herself for days, displayed no emotion at all. And Sundeep? He was still rapt in a memory, looking out at the garden, and maybe the cottage, with a lost look on his ravaged face.

The police officer they didn't know, from the nearest city it turned out, where they had taken the body for DNA testing, now cleared his throat importantly and pulled out a notebook. 'I hope you won't mind,' he said to Leela with the same theatrical pauses, 'if I ask Mr Sundeep a few questions.' 'Oh, but it is such a bad time for this,' Leela advised gently, yet, anyone who knew her could have sensed the steel in her words. But the man, oblivious to the niceties of estate life, persisted, beginning the harrumphing and hawing that preceded each of his questions. Leela looked imploringly at their local constable then, who had grown up on the estate himself, and held the whole family in awe. He waded in, drawn by old loyalties, 'But not today, sir? After all, what will poor Mr Sundeep remember of nefarious goings-on on the estate from so long ago? Men would drink and fight and do each other grave damage. Even the best employers could not have stopped them. Mr Sundeep, you rest, we will come back when the results are in,' he chattered, ushering his city colleague out at the same time. The latter wasn't happy, but allowed himself to be shown out, deciding that a less direct approach to uncovering the truth might work better next time. But there would be a next time, he assured Leela, as he left. Following behind him though, the local constable dropped his voice to reassure, too, 'But that next time will be as long as it takes for the results to make sense to us poor, befuddled estate constabulary.'

But no one in the big house needed the poor befuddled constabulary to tell them whose bones Sarge had found. There had been many deaths. Deaths of family members who had been ceremoniously laid to rest with many lovely things said about them by people who came from far and wide, but hardly even knew them. The help had died too; old retainers who had been given a dignified send-off, with more praise heaped on them than in life. Estate workers had dropped off like flies every summer when epidemics rose from the plains. Their farewells were more cursory. So deaths there were aplenty, but disappearances few. Sarj's vanishing into thin air had certainly raised eyebrows. But then they were reminded of what an irresponsible man he had always been. Had he done a day of work in his life? No. Had he spent any time looking into anyone's welfare? Well, no, not really, but in his sunny, easy manner with all, he had lifted everyone's spirits. He had glided through other lives, leaving a smile behind, but little else. So when he had left the estate, it had been explained away as much of the same drifting. And though he was missed, nothing had been done about it. But belatedly now, with the discovery of what was widely known to be a human skeleton, questions were being asked all over the house and estate and even in the town down the hill. Where had he gone? What had happened to him? Was it Sarj? Those who knew how the bones had been unearthed, nodded wisely to each other, and said, well, Sarge certainly thought they were special bones, and who would know better than that dog? These were the same people who had forgotten ol' Sarge as quickly as they had Sarj. Everyone was now in a lather to make the connection between the bones and the vanished Sarj.

At the house, having decided that the bones could only have belonged to Sarj, they had moved on to the next stage of the process. They felt baffled that they hadn't had an inkling, angry that such a terrible thing had been done to that affable man. Grief too was felt amongst a small handful who had genuinely cared. Sarge, most of all, with no beloved bones to bring back, appeared to want answers. He began to insistently hover at the door of the darkened room, occasionally letting out an imploring whimper, or a more imperious bark, when he could remember how. He was shooed away every time, or lured to the kitchen by the old cook with some meat. But inside the oppressive room, Sundeep wanted to talk without wasting any more time. Leela, putting it off day after agitated day, could no longer do so, and on a gloomy morning at the end of that week, finally relented. 'Tell me then,' she said to him, with resignation but with enough warmth, she hoped, to reassure him of her faith in him (in fact, wasn't she already sure of what his story would be?).

'It was a dark night. Like many dark nights on the edges of the estate, where life felt more primeval, emotions more close to the surface. Sarj had asked me to drop in for a drink, as if I had time for such things. I was, after all, running the estate single-handedly, with no help from him.' Leela almost stepped in to remind him that he had been given its sole ownership and could not have expected Sarj to be involved, but she bit her tongue and nodded to him to continue. 'He was sitting there, drinking as he always did. The dog at his feet. He was, in fact, already very drunk, and with slurred words, he prattled on about toads as big as elephants at the bottom of the hill, the sky looking green that morning, and how he'd found a brightly painted ball for Sarge in town. I was impatient and wanted to leave after my first drink, but then out of the blue, he said sorry. I was taken aback. I told him that I had most certainly blamed my uncle for a very stupid decision, but that I had never suspected Sarj of manipulating him. Whatever else Sarj was, he was neither sly nor furtive. He was an open and honest man who did not deceive. I told him this, and he looked even more shamefaced. It both shocked and intrigued me, never having known guilt to be an emotion Sarj felt; he was always just in the moment.

'I sat down and had another drink. Sarj then said he wanted to give the house back to me before he left. Where was he going, why and when? I had questions to ask and another drink was drunk. I have never been much of a drinker and I was not thinking clearly any more, or three steps ahead of him as I usually was. Then he started talking about not knowing how else to make reparations. To remove from my life the things I wouldn't want in it – things that caused me grief – and to give back that which was mine. I still didn't understand. Nothing had caused me grief other than the business with the house, and to call that grief was taking it too far perhaps. And he did seem to be saying he would give it back, which pleased me no end. But what would he take away? Him and his dog? Why was he finding this so hard to say? We had never been especially close.

'He then meandered into his plans for Australia, and I drank and drank from boredom and befuddlement. I got up to go when he started talking about training kangaroos to deliver packages, but he pushed me down in my seat with a desperation; a wild look in his eyes, both intent and imploring. The dog took fright at this in an unnaturally perceptive way and appeared to shrink to half its size. I, too, reacted with a reflexive tightening of my fingers round the neck of the bottle I was drinking from.' Sundeep looked shiftily at Leela then. Ready as he was to share the worst, he was hoping to find forgiveness in her face. But she looked different from when he had started the story. She looked distinctly alarmed, and this was unusual in a woman so tranquil. But there was no going back, so he pushed on with his story.

'"You must forgive us before we go though," Sarj had begged, "none of us will sleep easy again till we know you are at peace." "I forgive you," I said to him, with some exasperation. Where was the need for drama in all this, I remembered thinking? And said as much. "Come to the office in the morning," I instructed, feeling quite chipper, despite the unfortunate amounts I had drunk. I would finally get the house that was mine and be rid of both man and dog that had proven a nuisance. I had never disliked them actively, but they had been a minor thorn in my side always.

'He would be there, he said, and he thanked me for being so understanding. And then, he asked, would I mind if he took the estate car as there would be so much luggage? Sarj had never owned much, and I was startled by what I thought was his stated intention of taking things from the house. "But my god, you're like a dog with a bone! You won't actually let go, will you? You are giving up the house, but taking everything inside with you!" "No!" he shouted then, showing the first signs of anger I had ever seen him exhibit. "No, not everything," he climbed back down quickly and said apologetically enough, "only Leela." Then, he added so softly I almost didn't catch it, "And our boy."

'Something snapped inside me then, even as I heard a terrible thwacking noise. Again and again and again. Somewhere in the midst of all that, I remember throwing out the dog. It was still whimpering and running around in circles outside when the haze lifted. I took it back to the house first, because it refused to leave otherwise. There, I saw it melt away for the last time, hardly hearing or seeing it at all till last week. I went back to bury Sarj, in the dark patch under the eaves. Sitting on my haunches then, by the mound, I cried. Not over the loss of Sarj, but my family. The two I had thought to be my family. Two who had never been mine, just like the house hadn't come to me, because my uncle had never thought of me as his. It had all belonged to Sarj, and he wanted still more. He wanted to take it all as far away from me as he could. Snatching my dignity and self-worth from me at the same time. Yet, I'm the greedy one? He is the sunny, fey one who didn't care for things of this world? It was never about the house, Leela, now do you see?'

'I never knew,' she said. 'You didn't tell me either,' he countered. 'Secrets beget secrets,' he whispered, finally. 'And shadows other shadows,' she agreed, but softly to herself. Sundeep had the cottage sectioned off soon after on account of damp and great big shadows engulfed the estate, then the house, and then him; pushing him out of everyday life into the darkest corner of their home, with an inexplicable illness that ate away at him. But for some, she thought, looking out the window to see her son stride across the grounds with what was surely a large dog in his arms, there were no shadows and no secrets. They just see. Leela wasn't sure if she was one of those who could see the way forward with luminous clarity. As Leela watched, she was reassured that Sarge was still breathing. She understood that he was going on his last journey and that his son was taking him there as Hindus do. That journey would undoubtedly end where Sarj's had too. Which is what Sarge had been working towards all these years. Behind her, Sundeep's strained breathing was winding down as well. That last dose of medicine she'd given him, she had made extra potent, so he could rest. Peace at last for everyone, she thought. And for the first time in years, she broke into a smile.

THE LUST LIST

'Tom Hiddleston and Idris Elba walk into a bar ...'

Saira chuckled softly to herself. *She* was at a bar for a change. And didn't it look different! This one had sleek furniture, soft music and even softer lighting. So that even the most unattractive bar-goer might have half a chance of getting lucky. Bars did public service these days, who knew? More than two decades of devoted spousehood ago, when she was more likely to have been found at a bar, they were seedier and somehow more exciting. Of course, *everything* was an adventure back then. This evening's bar-propping didn't feel like something she had actually chosen to do. She was on a business trip to a city where she didn't know many. None she wanted to see, at any rate. When you've been married, raising children *and* holding down a job as long as she had, it required an enormous amount of effort to socialise with the not-so-much-in-synch, as people undoubtedly became with time spent apart.

But what when you grow out of synch, despite spending nearly every minute of every day with someone? She was thinking of Aman, her husband of twenty-five years, unhappily. But for what had transpired with him the weekend before this work trip, she would have been in her hotel bed by then, with a good book, face-timing with her uni-age children, and undoubtedly ending the night talking to him. As she had done for every one of her rare overnight trips in the last two decades. Him. At the end of the day it was only ever him. But *he* had cut her loose. Or at least that's what he magnanimously claimed he was doing.

'Don't you think,' he had said to her, running his fingers through his still thick shock of hair, in a manner that had never struck her as quite so affected before, 'we owe it to each other to make the most of what's left of life? Shouldn't we get out there and grab it by its balls? I literally mean balls, in your case. We married as college sweethearts and have been together ever since. How many have you seen other than mine? Let's enjoy what life has to offer before we are too old!'

She could hear the boiler hissing in the bathroom as his words sank in slowly. They had been dressing for a drink with friends when he'd sprung their new, unilaterally determined life plan on her. She put down the sensible beige top and trousers she planned to wear with extra care so he wouldn't see her hands shake. And then, said with even greater care so there could be no room for misunderstandings, 'Do you mean we should enjoy other people? Or let's be honest here, that *you* want to enjoy other people. By which you mean sleep with other women, because of course, we do enjoy the company of others, don't we?'

She hadn't been aware they weren't enjoying life. Living it to the full. Grabbing it by the short and curlies. And all those other clichés he had trotted out in the course of their hour from hell. They had rather a good life, she had thought. They got along, laughed together, lived well, had children who were thriving, occasionally made love, and gave each other room to grow. Was it in that room that he'd grown into someone else who wanted something else? She smoothed the beige/taupe/whogissashit ensemble back into her chest of drawers with greater fastidiousness than she'd selected them in the first place, noticing for the first time how boring they were. But the realisation barely touched her, just as his words were only sluggishly filtering through. She felt underwater, not-yet-surfaced-for-air slow and disconnected from the world around her, which seemed to have suddenly sped up and was threatening to leave her behind. Aman grimaced, mumbling something about how she always took things the wrong way.

'I mean, who doesn't desire other people, and lots of 'em, right?' she asked herself, swivelling half heartedly on the faux-leather bar stool two days and five hundred miles away from their life-altering weekend. She thought she had asked only herself, as the bar was half-empty. Of 'talent', totally empty, with no Elbas, Hiddlestons, or Cumberbatches in sight. Not even an ageing yet still scrummy Colin Firth. There was instead a group of much-the-worse-for-wear middle-aged men huddled around a table at the farthest end, grimly drinking their way through the bar stock. The likes of whom she had not yet resigned herself to, so she was glad they couldn't have heard her. But the youthful barmaid lifted an amused brow, as if about to answer. 'More gin?' she offered instead. She should keep her voice down, Saira reminded herself, if she didn't want anyone to think her discussions on sexuality with herself an invitation. Or a manifestation of madness! After all, she chortled, when has muttering to oneself ever been seen as alluring? Stealing a quick glance at herself in the long mirror behind the bar, however, she was glad to note that she looked nothing like the men of a similar age across the room.

But with the next sip of gin, she continued her interior (and sometimes not-so-interior) monologue. Aman and Saira had their Lust Lists like all long-term couples. Those inventories that were jokingly drawn up after the first decade of marriage, listing all the men and women they were allowed to screw without their partner walking out on them. Or even having the right to complain. After all, they'd have a list of their own where the same rules applied. And this list would get updated from time to time, and alluded to, and laughed about, often. But nobody took them seriously. Right? Why else pack it full of people you'd never meet, which was the accepted MO? Saira was as likely to meet 1. Hugh Jackman, 2. Denzel Washington and 3. The Downey, as Trump was to rule the world (But wait. That happened). It was an aide-de-fantasy and no more.

She was suddenly swamped by the memory of them curating their lists more than fifteen years ago.

'No, no, no,' Aman had insisted, 'you cannot have Sean Bean on your list. What if you bump into him when we visit our cousin in Sheffield next year?'

'Yeah, because Yorkshire is that small and I am that desirable.'

'But you are!' he had grinned, before gathering her into his arms and pulling her back into bed.

That was then though, and this is now. For the minutes she was lost in her memory, a smile had hovered around her lips. To be replaced with swimming eyes, which she wiped angrily, telling herself it was the gin, and a deep desolation as Aman's words from the weekend came back to haunt her. A desolation reinforced by the still-early emptiness of the hotel bar she was sitting in. Had she paid enough attention to his list, she wondered then. Had he snuck in people over the years that he was capable of bedding instead of sticking to those ordained inaccessible? Did it include the supermarket checkout girl she'd spotted him flirting with? Or the drunken neighbour at Janaki's party? Maybe even their daughter's seventh-grade teacher she knew he eyed up. Had he been spreading it about all these years?

Saira watched quite another liquid spurt out of the beer tap behind the bar as she weeded through what she knew. But even she knew there was no point in connecting the dots so many years later to discover whether she had been betrayed. Nothing but pain would come of that, she acknowledged. So she put those thoughts aside, actually clearing the air around her head with her arms, like she was swatting flies. That's all she wanted to feel about Aman now, that he was a mere annoyance; swattable, forgettable and very definitely contemptible. Looking around the room to ascertain she hadn't been spotted swatting invisible flies, she could see it had begun to fill up at last. What night owls people must be and how long had it been since she'd spent the night out on the town? Too long. There was something different about how people moved and watched and approached after a certain hour. She could see it happening to the people pouring into the bar. It was undoubtedly a popular pick-up spot, which she hadn't known when sidling in, but she was glad she was here to observe. Just observe. One scantily clad woman strode sinuously up to the bar to order strawberry daiquiris for all her friends. Followed by a cocky young man, breaking away from his pack to chance his arm. Saira busied herself with her tall glass of gin, but with her ears pricked. She had the feeling he was about to be shot down in flames and would rather not be seen enjoying it.

'I've seen you before, haven't I?' he tried. 'You're on that billboard two blocks down ...'

She rolled her eyes at her friends, before cooing, 'That billboard about single moms with problem kids? You're right, I am.'

It was when she swivelled away from the unfolding farce that she saw Elba and Hiddleston for the first time. Not so much Idris and Tom really, as Al and Mark. Pacino and Ruffalo, that is, or near enough. They had obviously come in with the sudden swarm of young people who must have been waiting for a silent signal from somewhere that now was the time to take over the city, now that the fuddy-duddies were safe in bed. As she would've been, curled around a good book, with her phone firmly to her ear, listening to her husband recounting his not-exactly-exciting day. But there was quite another conversation ringing in her head which the gin wasn't drowning out like she'd hoped.

'I'll have a Dark Horse,' said the tall one to the barmaid, naming the beer-de-jour. Yet, instead of giving the latter the once-over, as Saira would have expected, she was surprised to feel his eyes on *her*. It was delicious but of no conceivable use to her; she was on the verge of deciding when she was overtaken with an overwhelming urge to find out if it could be. Could this be the answer to her earlier question? Or even antidote (albeit fleeting) to her misery (also temporary, she was beginning to see)? If they didn't exactly set her imagination or anything else on fire, they were trim, well-groomed and looked robust (unlike the group still grouching in the corner). As Saira's epiphany progressed behind her experienced poker face, the man she thought of as 'Mark', detecting very little interest, took his beer to the table his friend had settled down at. It was distant enough to give her space, but close enough to keep her in his line of vision. Clever bit of positioning, she acknowledged, and her interest grew.

But not enough to silence the voices from the previous weekend still insistently arguing in her head. Aman had confirmed he intended to 'see others', still using euphemisms to, no, not cushion the blow for her, but just so he wouldn't feel bad about himself. The one thing he had never been able to do was accept his own failings. So, his next narcissistic tack (though this was the first time she'd put a name to his behaviour) was to blame her for the apparently sudden disintegration of their marriage, twisting things till it became about her – 'You know, we've come to this because you've been so preoccupied, so disinterested, so deliberately … undesirable.' She had gaped at that. Aghast. She'd borne babies, brought them up, looked after him, too, and then gone back to work, to bring her share of the bacon home. Through it all, through post-partum depression, the never-ending sleepless nights and many 'womanly' problems, she thought she'd managed to keep her end up. Literally. Having been an acquiescent sexual partner even at times she wasn't wildly interested. Then, he turns around and says *she* hadn't been up to scratch?

Well, she'd show him.

She sipped at her G&T, a little less decorously than before, stirring it with its miniature parasol swizzle stick, pinkie sticking out to show the watching boys she was still classy even when gulping it down. Should she do something, she wondered, to make her interest clear? She tentatively shifted on the stool to show more leg. With her dress hitched up enough to display still shapely limbs, she looked over at the young men to find them sitting up for a better look. While Mark was grinning openly at her, Al's body language, too, had become decidedly more come-hither (a phrase never used for a man, a corner of her brain registered). Yet, so unused had she become to the mating dance, that it made her feel distinctly funny, and she turned her back on them to order another calming drink and clock the reassuring presence of the seemingly sensible barmaid.

'Get that down you,' the girl urged, topping it up with a hint less tonic.

Saira agreed, feeling her somersaulting stomach, 'I think I shall need it.'

Next thing she knew, the men had moved several tables closer to her in a grown-up game of London Statue. Except that being still was no part of their plan. It was 'action' they were looking for, she told herself, as her resolve wobbled.

Because wasn't it Aman who wanted to 'throw their marriage open'? Yes, 'throw' he'd said, like baby and bathwater, down the drain. Some relationships aren't exclusive and that's fine, she reflected, as long as both partners are aware of that and have explicitly agreed to it. That wasn't their deal, and if that deal should change, could it be sprung upon her, as a given? That wouldn't be informed consent, the foundation of all respectful relationships, surely? But monkeys always hang on for dear life to the existing branch till they have a firm hold on the next. They want to eat their banana and have it too, she seethed. She would have had some vestige of respect left for him had he proposed a clean break, a divorce. And at that moment, as shock and blinding hurt turned into a cold anger, she knew she'd ensure that was just what he got. She was a romantic, she remembered telling Aman during their life-upturning argument, not a branch, nor a doormat. And not the prude he then accused her of being. SO not a prude, she thought, as she smiled back seductively at the Ruffalo-headed young man.

He walked up to the bar, leaving his friend behind, and sat down two stools away. So, we are still playing London Statue she thought. She slung a large swig of nearly neat gin down her throat in preparation. She was fairly certain she couldn't be bothered with game-playing any more. She was also sure her patience (or even her nerve) would run out if things didn't happen quickly enough now that she'd decided. Why should she wait? She suspected that her husband put this business of a free-for-all on the table all of a sudden, not because he wanted to get stuck in, but because he already was. Saira had nothing against the polyamorous, which she understood to be a lifestyle where people openly declare their multiple affiliations and do not keep partners in the dark. Very different, as far as she could see, from cheating. But she had known Aman almost all her adult life and knew he hadn't suddenly embraced a new lifestyle. No, if she knew him, he'd probably been cheating a while, and finding it inconvenient – all that subterfuge, extra expense and effort – he had decided to make it easier for himself. Little things that had gone unnoticed fell into place.

'But what was wrong with our old car?' she had asked, bewildered by the Corvette that had come home to stay. 'It was too small,' he said of the sedan he'd sold while patting his expanding waistline. At her incredulity, he had amended it to, 'I needed a change', and she'd put it down to that midlife crisis everyone was affecting. Just that his involved much more than his car.

It was her turn now. And that gave her a turn. Or she'd quite possibly drunk too much, but Saira attributed it to the lightness of being set free from a man who didn't deserve her. Nor did the young man waiting for her next move, but that was different. Feeling younger and more reckless than she had in years (anger and gin will do it every time, she admitted to herself, even as she squared her shoulders in readiness), she took the plunge. Plunging into her bag to fish out her room key, to hold it momentarily aloft so the young men got the message (now that she'd started, she wasn't taking any chances). She had, like all the guests, been given two sets when checking in and she was about to make the most of it. She did not intend to hand it to either of the men. How crass would that be, and how boring. She dropped it into her gin instead as she hopped off her stool, letting the bait hook the fish that was quickest to it. That the other man, Al, had moved up, too, hadn't gone unnoticed, and though she still preferred the taller, darker Mark, she didn't really mind who followed her back to her room. They both had melting puppy-dog eyes and from all appearances, taut bodies. What else would you need for a night on the tiles?

She sashayed past them both with equal indifference, though conscious of their eyes fixed on her every move, from her full lips on the long glass for her last sip of gin, to her hips swaying as she went. Flicking one last playful glance over her shoulder at her man-of-choice (just to tip the balance in his favour a little), she headed into the gloom of the dimly lit passages that led to her room, resolved not to look back till she had reached her destination. As Saira walked down the deserted hallways to total silence, she was initially disappointed not to hear his footsteps behind her, little knowing that the plush carpets in the long corridors were designed to absorb the clatter of footfall. But just when she'd decided that she would be glad of a quiet night after all, she heard a low whistle. Not a wolf whistle, no sane woman would ever respond to *that*. But low, sensuous and tuneful, unlike any whistling she'd heard before. For the first time since she'd started her long walk to freedom, she wanted to turn and see who was behind her. She had steeled herself, however, to walk on without a backward glance and she just about managed. Preserving the mystery till the last moment, she had decided, would be as important as the act about to be performed, and the climactic revelation of who it would be with more important than the crescendo to follow. It would be more exciting this way, she told herself, like the Russian roulette of romps.

The thought gave her saunter back an extra bit of slink. It had, after all, been ages since she'd felt this eager expectation, and well worth drawing out for that reason. This breathlessness. The fine hair on her arms prickling in excitement. Her stomach contracting with anticipation. But then, she heard something that made it more than contract, that made it lurch, and her footsteps falter. She nearly stopped to look around then, because the tune had just become more nuanced. Something had been added to it. The breath of another person. The whistlers began to harmonise as if they'd done it before. Two distinct strains, both low and tuneful. And chilling. Like the air piped out by snake charmers to hold their captive in thrall, it almost had her rooted to the spot. She knew she should turn around and confront them, tell them that that wasn't her intention. In fact, it wasn't her thing at all. But now she didn't want to look back at all, she was so afraid of what she might see. So she kept walking. Quickening her pace as the whistling faded, to run into her room. It wasn't until she was in its darkened interior, that she finally let out her breath, only to realise she could still hear the whistlers coming. Ever closer. She looked at her door and saw that she had left it ajar, exactly two-person wide. She waited then, ready for them.

THE SCARE

It had started with little brown envelopes and had progressed to the large Manila ones that were kept on a high shelf; a considerable stretch for a small man like him. But that had been half the thrill – the calisthenics involved in grabbing a handful of large, stubbornly unfoldable envelopes from way over his head, and then stealthily smuggling them, out of the close comfort of the storeroom, down the gloom of the long corridor, and finally out the door of their warren of offices. It had excited Arthur enough to send him scurrying to the bathroom to relieve himself the minute he got home. It gave him the rush of pulling off a heist. Or that shiver down the spine that comes with clandestine adventures in unknown places. The new place in this instance, was the shuttered room the stationery cupboards had been moved to, at the end of a passage he hadn't been down before. Tiny, with walls that appeared to close in on him, it was stifling and reassuring, all at once; the antithesis of the vast foreign shores he imagined he wanted to explore. Never having been farther than the next town, he couldn't be sure if it was the newness of these places that attracted him, or the distance from his old life.

Muddled longings aside, these were *Manila* envelopes. From a land recommended to him for its natural beauties, especially of the kind his mother would not have approved. It had been her habit to look piercingly at the brown women in their picket-fenced neighbourhood, more of whom arrived with every passing year, and say cuttingly, 'Those filthy coloured women! Look at the pestilence they bring.' And he looked, oh he looked, but he never got close enough to confirm the presence of pestilence. His mother had no more to say about it now, yet Arthur hadn't ventured forth. He had, perhaps in the end, agreed with her about pestilence, but not just emanating from *brown* women. Yet, he craved change. And something more, goaded by that familiar sneering voice, 'What will you do now? What can you possibly do?'

So, as a single man with a routine life, he indulged himself in exploits in his office instead. Getting his eager fingers into tight places and dark corners to prise out treasures like multicoloured post-its, satisfyingly clunky paper clips and, eventually, some fancy pens from China, fuelled his wandering fantasies, and fed his need to escape. China was another sensual chimera he'd never get near. But in taking those pens home, pens reserved for upper management, those Very Irritating Poseurs at work, in lining them up on his bedside table and stroking them with one finger as he drifted off to sleep at night, he felt a sense of triumph. And vindication. The path he'd chosen to free himself from his constraints, had been the right one after all. Even if the voice of constant doubt gnawed at him, stealing his peace. Clip-clip, clip-clip; it burrowed into him.

Naturally, the next step was staplers. But this highest prize amongst stationery pinchers was also the biggest challenge. Heavy, as well as unwieldy, they were nearly impossible to hide. Arthur got an extra thrill, therefore, in sidling out of work at the end of the day with staplers on his person. So close to his person, down the front of his pants, that he was afraid he might get a nasty nip in the process. But that was exciting, too. Like Russian Roulette, but without the glamour (and minus the mess, he noted happily, after his first foray). As for Russia, that stirred him as well. And *they* weren't brown, were they? It struck him as too large and chaotic a place, nevertheless. Too many people running about killing each other. Messy, and without any mopping up after, he decided, with a pleasing frisson of disgust. He was a fastidious man, pernickety about his daily rituals. Yet, he liked making the occasional mess, just so he could clean it up. And beating the rule-makers was a messy business, but one that had to be done, he'd concluded late in life. So, day after day, he worked his way through his employer's stapler stock (not forgetting to pocket boxes of bulldog clips and board pins alongside), till he'd nearly broken their stranglehold on office stationery.

He almost felt heroic, as a result. Not nearly as heroic as he'd once felt – just the once – when he'd stifled those scornful, probing whispers.

He decided he needed to take more audacious risks to revisit that high. Arthur started bringing lunch in because it provided him with a sizeable box in which to take office supplies home. More and more of them. The lunch itself was execrable, because now, of course, he had no option but to make it himself. Sandwiches with stale bread and cheap, watery jam, where he used to get a full, hot meal. Meat pies, or layered lasagnes, even Stroganoff once, he remembered, with an audible smack of his lips that made co-workers' heads turn and brows ruche. His mother had been an excellent cook, producing the kind of hearty fare that always went with a side order of badgering. The food he most certainly missed, though the heckling he could still hear as if he'd never put his foot down at all. At least there was no one checking his lunchbox at the end of the day any more, no one to peruse what he'd brought back home with pursed lips and bulging eyes, each conveying the fathomless disappointment felt in him, 'There, look, you've done it again! Or not done it. You never do get anything done, do you?'

This would be followed by the usual litany of ills that her martyrdom in the service of her son had brought her. Sometimes, these tirades had taken an ominous turn that quite frightened him. 'I brought you into this world, and it is I who keeps you in it. Oh ho ho, not just feed you and clean you and hide you behind my aprons when they come calling. Though you swindle, double-cross and wound me, I keep going and I keep you alive. You're hopeless without me. When I go, you will too. In the end, you'll see.' He had counted every second of these diatribes under his breath, wanting to tell her how much he loathed her, yet never daring to go so far. 'Mother,' he would have said, 'you dog my every step, make my life a living hell; it is the converse of being alive.' When finally, he felt it safe to tell her, she'd slipped away before he could. So, now, he counted the silent seconds after he opened his lunchbox and no hurtful harangue materialised out of thin air. Those rants had morphed into fleeting murmurs instead, more chilling because he didn't know when one would surface. He avoided the garden at night where voices had assailed him before. But never, fortunately, in his starkly lit drawing room, where he could eat the soggy sandwich left over from lunch, quietly, in celebration of the peace he had wrung from his situation and the stationery he'd brought home like a victorious crusader.

After having reached that pinnacle of purloinment, the cramped storeroom at the end of the once-abandoned corridor, lost its appeal. Its comfort had come from how it folded Arthur in, into a familiar foetal position, but now, he wanted to strike out and explore. He took to slipping other things into the capacious pockets of his super-sized trousers when no one was looking. Carrying them out in his blue-lidded plastic boxes at the end of each day. First, he targeted the gents' toilets, and though the tightness of the cubicles suited him well, most things were fixed to the floor and he came away with nothing but paper towels and corroded soap bars. Occasionally, the abandoned lighter. Altogether, his hoard from these raids were dissatisfyingly masculine. That didn't do as much for him, though he was comforted as well as diverted by this light-fingered double life, on the whole. Not much else about him, after all, could be described as light. His mother had reminded him often enough. 'For God's sake, Arthur, could you please not tread so heavily on the stairs, it does my head in' or 'You've been working in the garden? Really? Well, it hasn't done *you* any good!' But if she did realise in the end what did do him good, it was far too late, he thought with a smirk, as he looked out at his garden. *His* garden. Just before he was reminded – *And yet, you don't dare go into the garden at night.*

If he'd never had much to be proud of, he could at least lay claim to a talent for petty pilfering. It had, over the years, become his escape from the persistent reminders of his inadequacy. Stealing his mother's belongings – women's things – from under her beaked nose, had been exciting, on account of the exotica he snagged, but also scary as perdition, especially when he considered the consequences of being caught. No description fitted her quite so well as Harridan from Hell, Arthur pondered with a shiver. Nearly all his antics had ended in thrashings, because her beetling eyes rarely missed a trick. Especially *his* tricks. If he tried to run, she would catch up, lumbering and heavy though she was. But over time, he improved. Not at running away, but at evading detection. He learned to lie slyly and hide things in unpleasant places nobody ventured; from food in his underwear cupboard, to locks of hair and even nail clippings from the girls at school, secreted away in smoothed-over dips in the garden. These, he stole from the girls who mocked him, which was all of them, he realised later, but little did they know he'd extracted his pounds of flesh too. None of it was worth anything, however. There was very little of value in their house, too, as his mother preferred to salt it away rather than spend on him. So, every penny torn from her sausage fingers, every trinket she thought she'd concealed that he prised out, had been a victory for him. Possessing it all now, of which he reminded himself often, he felt incomplete still, and driven to fill that hole (yet, he reminded himself sharply, he did not regret putting an end to that old life).

When the attractions of the gents' loo failed to hold him, Arthur moved on to the ladies'. This was as good as visiting the glamorous places his colleagues went gallivanting off to. Only he could have become intimate with Manila, Shanghai and Moscow in his sorties into the office store, he recalled with some smugness. Was it any wonder that his explorations in washrooms yielded trophies by the truckloads (except that he didn't have trucks at his disposal, just lunchboxes and pockets)? He had helped himself to floral tissues, a few soiled with the imprint of lipsticked mouths, unfamiliar fragrant soap, empty perfume canisters and occasionally, if he was lucky, not-so-fragrant abandoned garments. It was while lifting the last, an unsavoury pair of somethings that he couldn't even name, that he felt observed for the first time away from his home. Had karma followed him to work? Was his moment of reckoning coming ever nearer? He set his sights on more challenging heists to soothe his unsettled soul. In the following days, he managed to pinch a couple of left-behind purses. It wasn't their money he wanted, but a peek into their world. He liked the feeling of punching an Arthur-sized hole (as if with a gargantuan office puncher; he'd snuck a few of those out, too) into someone's life and stealthily entering it. It was especially electrifying if it was a woman's. Particularly if it was one of those bossy ones always trying to rub his nose in his inadequacies. Every morning, as he settled down at his tidy workspace, he heard their buzz around him and knew they were raking over his many imperfections.

'He's unclean,' he thought he heard one whisper, 'I've seen him do dirty things behind the filing cabinet.'

'Really?' hissed another. 'Well, he's not coming near me. Not with those stains on his trousers.'

Arthur checked his pants nervously. There were stains, but they were inside. How did women always know of every chink in a man's armour?

'He's a fool,' laughed another. 'Doesn't he know I've seen him skulking in the ladies' loo? That I know every little thing he does?'

Looking around nervously for the source of this last voice, he realised it was his mother's.

Occasionally, however, very occasionally, he got the better of them. Because, although it was true, he'd felt

watched in the ladies' loo, he had never been caught. He
was glad, for example, that nothing had been said about
his removing his own underpants one day, when he had
found a particularly capacious pair that had been left
behind, and changing into them. On the whole, it was
another successful conquest and it emboldened him
considerably.

And so, after his incursions into the ladies' lavatories,
he set his sights on a woman he wanted to take down a
peg or two. His manager, Sally, that fussy, bossy harridan
who reminded him of his mother, simultaneously scaring
and angering him, was the one he wanted to humiliate the
most. Get inside her head so he could get back at her. Put
her in her place. Muffle her constant drone in his ears like
he'd managed, well, nearly managed, with his mother.

First thing in the morning, this harpy would start her
constant stream of complaints, 'Arthur, where is that report
I asked of you three days ago? Have you even started?'

Was it is his fault that the report had taken longer than
expected, because none of the material he needed was
in stock? None of it at work, at any rate. The womblike
storeroom wore a ravaged air, he noted, with some
satisfaction. But that wasn't all she harried him with.
There were also 'Arthur, do you even know what I'm
talking abouts' and 'Arthur, do you ever pay attentions?'
Oh, but he did pay attention. He had begun to watch her
very closely indeed, and had plans to get to know her better.

One frosty day, when the evening had drawn in quicker
and the chattering masses were leaving early for their

family homes and busy calendars of Christmas gigs, Arthur decided to stay back. As soon as he saw Sally step into the lift, he was in her office like a shot, without looking around properly, like the cautious man he really was. But excitement had got the better of him. Once in, he was disappointed to note that her sanctum was not the dive he had expected. Hoped for. Women, his scrutiny had taught him, were all secretions and protrusions, but this one was sadly tidy. Perhaps she had a cleaning fetish like his mother, which was a failing, too, he reassured himself, before moving to her neatly organised desk. He didn't know what he was looking for. He hadn't thought through what he meant to do. He just knew he wanted to do something that would so upset her, it would shut her up for a whole morning. Or, or, my goodness, he thought, maybe even send her home for the day! Could he actually pull it off?

He had opened up her desk drawers and begun to rifle through her belongings, stopping to finger a tampon here, or fondle a picture there. Which was when he found the photo of Sally in a wedding dress. He was taken aback. He didn't know she was married. Then, he looked again. Hard. Surely, the person in the white suit beside her was not a man? He felt a dawning sense of elation. Here was something nobody else knew. He had not heard any talk around the office. Sally was a fag and only he knew it. He found this incredibly stirring. He felt such a surge of electricity coursing through his fingers, from the picture he was gripping tightly, and back, that he was afraid he would damage it. But he was also not afraid. Let her know that he knew! That the tables had been turned and Arthur had her in his power now. His hands trembled with anticipation. That little tic beside his eye had begun to jump. But just when he decided he should sit down and calm himself before taking that big next step in the Undoing of Sally, he heard a noise.

Arthur was definite there wasn't another living soul in their office. He had seen them all lope off home. But then, he heard it again, and it was nearer this time, which sent him into a bit of a funk. Was he about to be found out just as he got to the most satisfying part of his year-long explorations? As he neared the climax he was denied nearly all the time, by malicious interlopers? Or interloper, as it had been, but he shook that idea from his head. *Hadn't he made it impossible?* About to look sensibly into the possible source of the clumping noise, he felt a puff of wind on the back of his neck. It was a familiar puff of wind, laced with a murmur he had heard before, and he didn't need to know any more. Dropping the picture, and without stopping to check what else he'd left askew, he ran. He ran down the stairs and out the front door of the undeniably deserted building. He ran past the bus stop and all the way home. It took him double the usual time, but only while he ran did he think he could outrun his fate.

In the cold light of day, while taking the bus to work (now that Destiny wasn't on his tail any more), he felt rather foolish. He decided he had misread the portents of the night before. Sally, of course, was to blame. There was no doubt he was meant to take her down. He had felled a giant before, and the Universe knew it and wanted him to repeat the feat. It would be another vital step towards stopping this march of harpies that sought to take over the world of meek men. So, he bided his time at work again, humming and smiling to himself, to the surprise of those who were used to his habitually glum face. Sally, herself, did the rounds of their desks a few more times than usual, looking searchingly into each face, nearly gasping aloud at the expression on Arthur's. Yet, if Sally seemed unsettled, so was he, and he decided that he wouldn't wait till everybody had left like the previous evening. He would mount his attack the minute Sally decamped with a few of her closest cronies. Just after five, when the lights around Sally's section had dimmed, he made his way purposefully into her well-ordered office again. Everything was back in its place, he noted, with frustration. He rummaged through the drawers, his heart sinking at the thought of her having taken the precious photo home. And then, he found it. It was tucked away at the back of the bottom drawer. Obviously, she had underestimated her adversary, thinking he wouldn't try again. Imagining he wouldn't find the picture of her flagrant lesbian liaison because she'd hidden it with greater care. He turned the phrase on his tongue with a shiver of revulsion that turned into delight when he realised he could finally do what he'd been planning for the last forty-eight hours. There were no clumping noises today to scare him away. No murmurs around his ears, warning him off. The time was nigh. He placed the picture carefully on the desk and got on tiptoe, till he was hovering over it. Then, when he'd positioned himself just right, he unzipped his fly.

That's when every light in the office blazed back on. As Arthur jumped back in fright, he saw Sally staring at him from the doorway with her hand on the switch. Luminous, in the glare she'd just exacerbated, she looked like an avenging angel, the look of horror on her face changing swiftly to triumph, and then incontrovertible contempt. She had that sneer on her face he'd seen every day growing up. As he fumbled ineptly with his zip, almost trapping himself, she came to a halt just before him. While he went an apoplectic red, Sally, who should have been seething, remained calm, even smiling, if with more disdain than any other woman had looked at him. And plenty had. But most of all, she seemed to have no intention of speaking. Not a word sprang from her in that long, humiliating moment as Arthur first looked at her with terror, then found his lips zipped as tightly as he'd ensured his fly was, belatedly. She did not take the opportunity to castigate or belittle. He had thought she would whine, complain, and he would take the higher ground then. Tell her she was a bitch, not fit to lick his boots, who should get off his case, then and forever. All the pent-up cut and parry he'd managed to squeeze in, in that one last-gasp opportunity with his mother, he'd give vent to, all over again. Instead, his middle-aged harpy of a manager looked composed and thoughtful.

Looking into her face, which was unbelievably settling into an almost kindly expression, several thoughts chased through Arthur's fulminating mind; from the fact that she'd clearly been lying in wait for him, to remembering the feeling of being watched in the women's washrooms, and wondering if that had been her, too, to fury at the bizarre treatment she was meting out to him. Fury that she wasn't putting him through worse, so he could lash out like he only felt able when driven to the most extreme anger. Which brought the utmost relief. Joy, even. Like he'd known only once in his life. The one time he'd mustered the courage to fight back. That surge of adrenaline that'd rushed through his veins was addictive, and stealing never quite replicated it, but he so desperately wanted to feel it again. So, he waited, but nasty bitch that she was, she withheld that joy. And that almost constant feeling of defeat – to this woman, to all women, to the world – seeped back into every sinew of his body. As his body gave way, his tongue loosened and his bladder, too. And that deed, which he meant to do all over the evidence of her shame, to show his deep contempt, and to mark his territory at the same time, to show her who was boss, happened very differently indeed.

'Oh, Arthur. Oh god, Arthur!' Sally exclaimed with dismay and pity, as he unmistakably soiled himself, standing rooted beside her desk. 'Here, let me help you,' she suggested, as he sank to the ground and cried. She rummaged through the same drawers he had been pawing earlier to find some paper towels. He cried even harder as she handed them to him, instructing him to hold them strategically as he made his way to the gents'. He wanted to tell her not to kid herself. Not to imagine for a moment that she was responsible for his humiliation. That it was, in fact, all of them. The whole world of women ranged against him, mocking him. But most of all, one woman, whose lifelong contempt for him sent an icy finger of shame down his spine in that moment, in which he lost control. He didn't say any of that though, instead, he blubbered his contrition as he cowered before her. No longer able to get his sticky fingers into her affairs, he turned his palms submissively upwards. As if in supplication. As if it was his mother looming over him with her cane.

He was craven. 'I was just looking at it. I wasn't going to ...'

He pleaded for mercy. 'Please. You must give me another chance. You are an understanding woman. I have always thought so. Please don't take a poor man's living, I beg you!'

And with his customary venom coming through for a moment, 'Not when you have so much to lose yourself!'

All the ignominy he had expected her to heap upon him, he brought down on himself. But Sally did not mean to hold him to ransom forever like his mother had. There were no threats of 'Try that again, why don't you ...' and 'Do this or I'll ...'. In fact, all that was left was her flustered sympathy at his embarrassment. And only in the end did she offer both reassurance and a warning in response to his timorous query about calling the police. 'No,' she promised, 'I won't, on this occasion. But only because you've punished yourself enough, already ...'

Arthur slunk away then. Back to his shared workspace, with the inevitable ignominy of everyone looking at him and knowing what he'd just done. Smelling what he'd just done. Especially the women, wrinkling their noses delicately as if they never did dirty things. He knew better. He'd haunted their bathroom for weeks. He imagined them tutting and tittering to each other, 'Didn't I tell you he was dirty?' 'No mistaking that stain in his pants this time!'

He headed for the toilets. Deciding to relieve himself in the women's lavatories and feeling better for it, he took his time heading back out. After all, he'd had quite the scare. And Sally would undoubtedly be waiting for him. Sally and her pack. Making him feel, as always, on his own against the world. On the other hand, he had begun to suspect *she* was in here. With that almost constant presence watching him in this loo, he had never felt alone, even if he wasn't sure he liked the feeling. That creeping panic that his past would catch up with him, which had never quite left Arthur over that long year of smothering it, was on the verge of reaching fever pitch. But even as he weighed up the relative merits of the devil against the deep blue sea, he was suddenly alerted to a presence *outside* the washrooms. There was footfall. And voices, primarily male voices. In that moment, he knew that it was all about to come to an end; this new life he had eked out from the old, which included his fresh spate of escapades. He'd never be allowed anywhere near another ladies' loo again, obviously. Or even ladies themselves, perhaps. Or around anyone or anything that he might attempt to pocket, possess or subdue. He felt then the same mixed emotions he had always felt when contemplating a lady-free life – fear and a kind of exhilaration, all at once. He had a strong hunch that that's what was waiting for him outside.

'Is he in there?' boomed one man, while the other could be heard addressing the gathering throng in the corridor, 'Stand back, there's a miscreant inside and we're going in.'

'But he isn't dangerous,' he thought he heard Sally say, 'just mixed up. Let me talk to him.'

'Where we're taking him? No one's gonna talk to him.'

At which, Arthur rushed out to embrace the life that was coming for him, running straight into the arms of a burly policeman. They pinned him to the wall outside the washrooms, while his colleagues scattered to make room for the drama that had so propitiously lit up a dull afternoon. Who knew Arthur was so exciting? 'He's a minor league pervert,' Sally was still fighting his corner, 'and a thief, at worst.' She looked imploringly at him, as if she cared whether he spoke up to clear his name. Swatting this unlikely thought away, he hung his head to resist the temptation to deny his crimes, to bleat for mercy, or any of the things that life under his mother's thumb had taught him to do.

The more loquacious policeman stated, instead, 'We've been watching him for a while and he's more than that, ma'am. He's been stealing you blind. Hundreds of boxes of stationery from this office! Post-its, paper clips, staplers ...' His colleague looked at him with annoyance as he ticked a long list of items off his fingers, and ceased paying attention. But Arthur was listening intently, as if it was important that they had found everything he had ever put away.

'And for these,' Sally interrupted, testily, 'you are hauling him off? Why, I can deal with this myself.'

But the handcuffs were already out, being placed with ceremonial deliberation on Arthur's wrists. And still, he didn't protest. Still, he didn't pour forth the denials, excuses of having led a deprived life, or pleas for clemency everyone was expecting from him.

'The trail of thefts from your office, madam, led us to his house, which we have searched with a fine-tooth comb,' said the one with the gob.

'You with a comb,' his colleague grumbled, under his breath then, 'the rest of us used modern techniques.'

'Every last inch,' continued the garrulous one, 'all the way to the bottom of the garden.' Looking directly at Arthur when he said that, he was disappointed to find neither guilt, nor remorse, or anything but willing resignation writ large on his face. The policemen smiled wearily. They had come across many a sly little man like him before, simultaneously frightened by the consequences of their actions, yet perversely pleased by them too. This one, decided the quieter officer, having had the time to observe his quarry, was waiting for something more than this long list of stolen items. 'We've found ...' the other held forth for Sally's benefit, now that the crowd had begun to disperse, put off by the longwinded tale of minor misdemeanours that seemed to involve nothing more swashbuckling than stationery. Arthur, himself, so keen minutes ago to find out exactly how much the policemen knew, no longer seemed interested in the battery of accusations being brought against him. Instead, he stared glassy-eyed at something in the distance behind the fuzz, appearing at the same time to shrink from it. 'Every last item from this office,' the chatty cop continued, 'we found in boxes, buried by his wall. Box upon box upon box, covering every inch of the bottom of his garden, shoring something up, holding something down. All thinly concealed, with a layer of hand-smoothed soil.'

But even as the other officer signalled impatiently for him to hurry the story along, Copper A carried on, 'Digging further down, we hit pay dirt. We found the one other thing we suspected he'd interred there.'

'Because underneath it all,' interrupted the second officer, before his partner could lose his way in elaborations, 'was a much bigger box ...'

As his office mates leaned in again, all agog at the turn the story was obviously about to take, Arthur's eyes widened, too, and his face blanched, but he wasn't listening to the policeman's account. He knew it already. 'When we opened the big box,' the raconteur in blue continued, 'there wasn't swiped stationery there, nor odious items from the washrooms, BUT there was a smell. An overwhelmingly bad smell.'

As the listeners recoiled obligingly, at just that second, Arthur twitched too. The twitch then became a tremor, as he continued to watch that *something* in the distance.

Everyone else in the office, however, was huddled around the policemen, rapt, and the gratified officer pushed ahead, 'Once past that bad smell, we found layer upon layer of paper products. It was like playing a nasty, noxious game of Pass the Parcel. Sifting through it all, we found a large manila envelope. Stained and packed solid.'

'Inside,' pronounced the policeman as the crowd held its breath, 'was a head.' Sally, who had been standing by Arthur to show solidarity, yelped and ricocheted away. But Arthur didn't care. He could just about spy the door to his old haunt, the small storeroom, down the deserted corridor nearest Sally's office, and he fancied he saw the doorknob turn slowly. 'And then, we found the rest of the body. A very large, decomposing body in a floral smock. A body, whose worn-away fingers still gripped a recognisable cane. Your mother's body, I presume, Arthur?' questioned the officer archly, as he focused his full attention for the first time on the deathly pale, perspiring face of their captive. In what resembled slow motion, wild-eyed Arthur finally opened his mouth to speak, and a pin-drop silence descended around him, as every witness to the unfolding drama awaited the grisly admission of his irrefutable guilt.

When Arthur spoke, however, it was not with the voice of a man, but the terrified squeal of a little boy, 'I thought it was. My God, how I wish it were so. I did everything I could to keep her there. But she wouldn't stay! She hasn't stopped yammering in my ear even once. Constantly reminding me that she would come for me. And now she's following me around, too.'

The policemen stifled a smile as Arthur broke down, 'You must believe me. All this. All this was to get your attention. I wanted you to find me. I needed you to take me away before she could. Oh, I so desperately wanted that!'

And then, with the wail of a man at the end of his rope, 'But it's too late now, too late. She kept her promise. She's come for me!'

'Look,' he said then, and as every eye followed his tremulous finger to the shuttered room at the end of the passage, they saw the door swing open.

FULL CIRCLE

The usually gloomy Bosworth Drive community hall had been transformed by a dozen large chandeliers, loud music, and even louder voices hailing each other in hearty Bengali, into a mela. Except that it wasn't so much a mela as a pujo. A pujo, mind you, not a puja, Yana reminded herself in that exact finger-waggling manner Putul 'Aunty' had, and hid a little smile. A puja is worship of the gods, Biplob Uncle had explained in his pantomime villain way (twirling his moustache and booming at her jocularly), but a pujo is living it up like the gods.

Pujo, anywhere in the world, means getting up at the crack of dawn to slokas sung in a gravelly, just-outta-bed voice. For Yana, it meant gathering at the festive hub of the community hall bright and early for the most enormous breakfast anyone had ever seen. Luchi, aloor dom, even prawn kochuri if the aunty in charge of the kitchen had woken happy. *And* the most mouth-watering range of soft, squidgy, syrupy sweetmeats ever served outside Bengal. That was just the start. For the rest of the day, the hall would fill with music and games and as much chatter as could be squeezed in, making up for months of maintaining a stiff, very British upper lip (which even the British no longer bothered with; not since Diana's death, Biplob said). Lunch would see a mind-boggling array of delicacies, from paturi – spicy fish baked in banana leaf – to patishapta – sweet coconut and cream filled pancakes. And all this was just a prelude to the evening's revelry!

'First you eat, and then you eat again, then you gossip, and (sometimes without being asked) sing until your jaw clacks loosely, and your belly grows so large from all the food, it obstructs your vision and makes you believe your singing is going down well,' Biplob's brother, Subir, said with that same twinkle in his eye. Clean-shaven as he was, there was no opportunity to twirl a moustache. 'And then you repeat it all, till you're round enough to roll home at the end, promising yourself to never do it again, and yet you do!'

The Bengalis of Leicester were her mother's folk. Her own people really, but she never thought of anyone as hers except Mom. They were every bit the bombastic (though often in ways that mocked themselves, Yana thought, looking over at Biplob and Subir) gourmand-bibliophiles they were said to be. Here, in the hastily but expensively rigged hall, they gathered under ceilings dripping with crystal, jostling for the best view of, or selfie with, a magnificent idol of the mother goddess Durga. Her ten mighty arms held weapons used to defeat evil and dispel darkness. And boy was she doing the latter! The glare from Durga's arsenal added to the brilliance of legions of fairy bulbs and animated illuminations, lighting the rounded Bong faces already incandescent with excitement up further.

Because this could almost be Ballygunge and not Bosworth Drive at all. *Dada, Boudi, kemon accho, kotodin dekha hoyni*, they greet each other because it's the thing to do, though they'd gathered for Rabindra Sangeet only the Sunday before. At pujo time, however, it isn't just the usual suspects. Not merely those who warble in the gloom of the old hall in the quiet of the weekend. At pujo, they descend from all around. Bengalis who live in areas without pujos. Bengalis who live in areas *with* pujos from which they've been excommunicated for arguing about Tagore or Ray. And even Bongs at the heart of their communities, pivotal to their own pujos. They descend on other pujos to check out the competition and greet their frenemies, as is customary at that time of the year. But most of all, to try the food. To shovel it down and find it wanting. In reality, it would be 'tip-top', but how could members of rival pujos possibly admit to that? How could they acknowledge that the rosogollas, no matter which pujo they sampled them at, always took them back to their rose-tinted youth in Calcutta?

'A rosogolla is a juicy, sponge-ball Tardis,' Biplob beamed at Yana. 'They turn back time like nothing else can.'

Yana smiled back queasily. As much as she loved the syrup-ball time machines he was extolling, she had been force-fed one too many of those bombs. At least ten that evening alone. She appreciated the kindness of those who stuffed her with food, and told her vastly embellished but hugely entertaining stories of the 'old days' in Calcutta, but the city of her foremothers was distant, magical *and* completely unreal. Now with her stomach overfull, and the lights whirling uncomfortably, this world was beginning to slip away too.

She made a break from the circle in which she stood. A circle full of raconteurs, so rapt in their tales, none of them noticed her inching away. Stumbling through the hall in her badly-pinned and much-too-long sari, she eased herself into the cool darkness of the porch (but not before running the gauntlet of aunties offering more food). It appeared deserted. Too cold for most British Bengalis, Yana realised, thinking of all the uncles lost in the layers they wore to venture out-of-doors, with the infamous monkey cap perched atop. She breathed in the frosty air to calm herself. These festive gatherings could get too much for her after the initial whirl of colour and excitement. When that sense of belonging ebbed, a disconnectedness would often take over, like an out-of-body experience. Like right then. Whose body was that looking lumpy in sparkling silk, Yana thought. Whose sari was that snagged between those legs in that unseemly manner?

She had a Plan B, however, and it was in the porch. Sneaking behind the tottering pile of coats and hats deposited there, she started unravelling her six (though it felt like sixty-six) yards of shimmer. Impatient with the pace of its unwinding in an untidy but opulent puddle at her feet, she pulled it out in clumps, unpinned in a hurry, and then stood there in her underlayers, wondering where on earth her back-up bag was. 'But I left it here!' she mumbled anxiously. But *here* it wasn't. She took in the silky carnage around her disconsolately, because she knew she wouldn't be able to put it back on. She would either have to freeze to death in the porch of the poxy community hall, and make the front page of the *Bosworth Probashi* the morning after, or worse still, she'd have to pull on the tobacco-tainted and perfume-soaked coats and hats of the uncles and aunties inside to keep warm. But as she contemplated this fate-worse-than-death, with the degree of disproportionate gloom only a tween can concoct, Yana heard footsteps approaching. Relieved at first, she was struck by the thought that being found in her underwear on such an auspicious occasion may not go down well with the more sanctimonious reveller. A more metaphorical but as mortifying a dressing-down might follow. She tensed as the footsteps got nearer, followed by a rustling amongst the coats and hats. Running through her mind were the things she might say to explain her déshabillé and discomfiture. But just as she'd decided that kung fu fighting her way out was the answer, yes, even in her voluminous petticoat and conical blouse, a flurry of chiffon and flyaway hair much like her own crashed through. And it was just the person, no, the *only* person, she wanted to see – it was Mommy!

'Here you are! I was looking for you everywhere. Look, I found your bag abandoned on the floor. You need it now, don't you? I knew you wouldn't want that on long. Look at mine! It's halfway down my knees already!'

Mommy meant her sari and not upper-body parts, which she complained about too sometimes. But the breathless, runaway-train manner in which she discussed *everything*, made her mother seem more like thirteen than thirty-six, which reassured Yana, even as it made her laugh.

'Well, anyway,' continued Mommy as she wound up the discarded sari, while Yana slipped into everyday gear, 'I've had enough of this shindig. You coming?'

They set off into the crisp autumn night, with a sky full of stars nearly outshining the blaze from the hall. Yana loped along contentedly, as she was never happier than when it was just her and her Mom. Especially at these events, where it wasn't long before the latter too would give up the ghost of trying to fit in. 'Mommy Misfit' she laughingly called herself. Also 'Stealth Mommy' for the talent she'd just displayed in spiriting them both away. Yana giggled at the thought and laced her fingers through Mommy's in the easy camaraderie they shared. Then she said, rather wistfully considering her fit of giggles just minutes before, 'I was having fun at first. Then I felt alone. Like always. Like you do. It's you and me against the world, Mommy.' Mommy dropped a kiss on Yana's head, but when Yana looked up at her, her mother's brow was furrowed.

Since that night, six months ago, Mommy hadn't been around as much. For all of twelve years, she had always been home to help Yana with her homework and join the family for dinner. But Yana knew it was for her that her mother never went anywhere in the evenings or worked the longer hours that might have propelled her up the career ladder. Mommy always said she *wanted* to be there for Yana. So what had changed? How had she pushed her mother away? Yana didn't think these amounted to abandonment anxieties, yet she couldn't ever completely disregard the fact that her father had never had anything to do with her. Mom never talked about him. But Yana understood reproduction well enough to know she was bound to have had a Dad at some point. That, however, was the least of her concerns now.

'Is Mommy back, Dida?' she asked that evening, looking around the table. 'Na, Buri,' replied her uncharacteristically concise grandmother. And the spinach and cottage cheese dish that was her favourite on winter evenings wilted, along with her spirits.

'Can you come to my after-school club tonight, Mommy?' Yana asked her one morning. 'It's parents' evening. You always come.' But Mommy looked thunderstruck and mumbled unhappily about having made a prior appointment. Then with an apologetic squeeze and a kiss, a rustle of crisp cotton and the faintest whiff of mild perfume, she was gone. Till past Yana's bedtime!

When she was in, she seemed distracted. She would spend hours on the net, searching, but she wouldn't say for what. They would sit side by side as they always did, but instead of chatting and laughing and discussing their world, her mother appeared to have entered another one. 'What are you looking for, Mommy?' to which Mommy would smile and shrug, until one day she admitted it was an old college friend she was seeking. Someone she had lost contact with more than a decade ago. All very strange, Yana thought, because she'd never looked back before. In fact, she was a distinctly forward-looking Momma, dodging questions about the past and turning them into jokes until Yana forgot, amidst the laugher, what she'd wanted to know.

So, now, to deflect the hurt and draw entertainment from this new situation like her mother had taught her, Yana began to think of the many ways in which you might lose your closest friend. Sliding like small change down the back of the sofa was her favourite, especially for petite peeps like her mom, but in Dida's swampy payesh was just as likely (though no way would she say that to Dida). And how about the pages of her books, into which she sometimes thought her mother would gladly dissolve? Though never before this had she considered that Mommy might want to melt away without her. They were BFF's after all! Like the terror she'd felt as a toddler watching bathwater disappear down the drain; she had a horrible sinking feeling that she was about to lose the only person in the world she loved. Fused to her heart and joined at the hip, they were the Two Musketeers – Yana and her mother-in-arms.

She did have friends she hung out with at school. But they teased her sometimes, calling her Lizard

Lass and, worse, Geeky Gecko. But she had always had Mom to come home to. Mommy who would say, 'Those are artist's fingers, my darling. They are meant to be different.' Yana would then beam at her with all the love in the world and get back to her watercolour or pencil sketch. In the morning, the picture would be up on the noticeboard in the kitchen, reserved just for her creations. They were excellent, everyone agreed, and that made Yana forget her 'freaky fingers'. 'No, no, magic fingers!' Mommy would insist. Until two nights ago, when she said instead, 'I know someone else who draws like you.' And Yana thought her heart would break – 'I'm not enough any more.'

Most of all, she was really and truly baffled. After less likely possibilities like Mommy having been replaced by a partybot were put away, and the early onset of some form of senility considered, she plumped on Mommy having developed a dual identity as a superhero. This was the best possible solution to the mystery, but also the most improbable, as Mommy was tiny and slender and unlikely to be able to take on Bane or Mr Freeze. Or even the willowy but tall Poison Ivy. Still, you never know, Yana thought hopefully. What she *did* know was that she wasn't the only concerned family member.

She overheard Grandad, or Dadu, state with exasperation one day, 'Bhimroti aabar dekha diyechhe dekchhi.' To which Dida responded crossly, 'Timothy! Ebaar support koro oke. Not only Anika but Yana will be affected this time. So why not start with grasping his name?'

Yana didn't get that. Oh, she got most of the Bengali bouncing back and forth between Dida and Dadu daily, even the reference to senility (which had triggered *that* worry), but it still didn't make sense.

Bradford-based visiting uncle (the only real one), Amit, too had something to say. This time, directly to her mother. 'What do you think you're doing?' he prissily questioned Mommy when their paths crossed on the upstairs landing. 'It's a far, far better thing I do ...' Mommy tossed over her shoulder as she ran down the stairs lightly. If her mother was still quoting from her favourite books, thought Yana, she hadn't been replaced by a robot after all.

Then one day, out of the blue, her Mom announced that Yana was coming too on one of these new Mommy jaunts. This led to a rather stormy dinner that Yana watched unfold, bemused as well as amused.

'If it didn't work then, it won't now,' Dadu said dismissively.

Mommy mostly refused to get drawn – part of the reason she'd been skipping family meals – but now she replied evenly, 'We are older, Baba.'

'Older. But are you wiser? And what about us? And Yana?' he grumbled, throwing everything he could think of into the argument. All except his usual sarky query of 'Does the postman have to know?' Perhaps he thought this time the postman already knew. Yana had to stifle a giggle.

'It has NOTHING to do with you. It never did, which you don't seem to understand. As for Yana,' Mommy now beamed, 'this is ALL about her. *Her* big adventure.'

Dida twinkled at Yana as the latter caught her breath. She couldn't be more at sea, and a very choppy sea it was too. Were they going deep-sea diving then? Mountaineering? Camping? No, none of these were Mommy things to do. Glamping then, maybe. Or, perhaps they were going to meet George Clooney, though Yana couldn't imagine why she should be dragged to that and not one of Mommy's swooning friends. Perhaps it was Ol' George after all, because Dadu complained about Mommy's 'choices' more than usual, and Dida was clearly exceedingly excited (perhaps Mommy should take Dida along instead). The latter took to insisting Yana have a bath *every* day. She even hung around Mommy as she dressed for the BIG event, giving Yana a tiny bit of a reprieve from her constant surveillance that week.

'Why not wear the maroon and gold sari?'

Mommy rolled her large kohl-rimmed eyes, 'This is not pujo, Ma. It's a quiet evening with a friend.'

That would explain the absence of camping kit or scuba gear, Yana decided. Mommy didn't even seem to be carrying a George Clooney poster for an autograph. She knew some women had famous people sign their breasts and seriously hoped Mommy wasn't planning to do that. But despite her attempt to exude cool, Mommy did seem more flustered than usual. In taking turns with Dida to uncharacteristically cluck over Yana's sticky-up hair and her way-too-weird clothes, she betrayed her nerves, Yana felt. So she almost-graciously flounced off to change into the orange mini dress Mommy wanted her to wear. It picked out the strange ginger strands that had always streaked her jet-black hair. Which she slicked down now to Dida's approval. But she drew the line at wearing dainty shoes. How did it even matter, she wondered, how *she* dressed for this do?

They ran laughing to the end of their road, to catch the bus to town. 'The Two Musketeers ride again,' Yana whispered under her breath happily. Riding and falling over, as the bus jerked to a stop in front of a row of shiny modern buildings in the centre of town, they dusted themselves down and took in the imposing glass facades in front of them. 'Three Sons of York Art Gallery' said the fancy-pants sign on the middle building. 'Art?' marvelled Yana and her heartbeat quickened. Entering the establishment, they climbed past the swanky studios to the skylit ones at the top. Stepping into the last long corridor in the clouds, and breathing in the scent of turpentine and late afternoon spring sun, Yana felt a sense of completion she'd never known before. It was the excitement of being surrounded by art, which she worshipped, but there was something more.

Mommy took a deep breath outside a set of swinging doors, and taking Yana's hand, led her in. They wove their way through an Aladdin's Cave of Wonders, filled with the metallic gleam of mechanical installations, the iridescent colours of canvasses drying in the sun, and the actually audible groan from tables weighed down with paints and brushes and chisels. Yana had to be coaxed along, she *so* wanted to scrutinise everything she could see. Till the Genie of this magical lair stepped out of the shadows before them, and her attention was snagged. Here was something more intriguing still – her usurper in Mommy's life. She knew it without being told. She willed herself to feel resentment but found she couldn't. She was transfixed instead.

Having emerged from the shadows, the Genie stood in a spot of sun streaming in from the skylight, smiling warmly at Mommy (like he wasn't a djinn at all, but Aladdin beholding his Jasmine). Then, he turned to look at Yana and a shock ran through her. Her Mom, never-at-a-loss-for-words Mommy, was standing stock-still and silent too, as if electrified. As if the world outside their tiny crackling circle had ceased to matter. Then, the Genie's face creased into another warming smile, but this time it deepened, further and further till it became incandescent. And without knowing it, Yana smiled that same dazzling smile back at him. Then she laughed, because his hair in the sunshine was a fiery ginger, like it had been set on fire. Echoing the odd ginger streaks in her own. But he was pale and pearly to Yana's glowing caramel. He was a surprise and he wasn't. 'An artist to learn from, Yana,' Mommy was saying softly, 'and a friend.' 'Of course, a friend,' the ginger djinn rumbled, reaching out to take her hands in his large ones. Yana of The Humongous Personal Bubble found herself entrusting them to him.

And as she watched with wonder his big, square-tipped, splayed fingers with interstitials that could be webbing, wrapping around her small, square-tipped, splay-fingered hands, she understood everything.

Daddy Lizard. And the Third Musketeer. OMG.

THE LITTLE THINGS

The bit Raima liked best was lying in the comfort of his arms. The crook of his arm, the pillow of his greying chest, the curve of his chin under which she could tuck her dark head were the most important parts of his body to her. As were her limpid eyes to him, her light voice, her arms wrapping around him tenderly. What they had was a very comfortable intimacy which did not always end in sex. But they liked to get naked and touch skin to skin. 'Ahhh, that nonchalant nakedness again,' she would sigh, smiling up at him, and he would respond by covering that smile with his own. His mouth might then find its way down to her breasts, no longer pert after several children, but still eminently kissable. And so he would. Even stopping to flick his tongue into her surgically-mangled belly button, another relic of prodigious reproduction. He would bury his face in her next, breathing her in and licking her out. But all this was a prelude to what pleased them most – the talking. Talking for these two wordy souls was the only logical climax to their coming together.

'So, Bobby will see you in April?'

'Yes, and I shall meet him armed with books. And fish! You know how he loves his fish.'

'Oh, but don't we all?' said the girl from the Gangetic delta wistfully.

Then there'd be more about food, or books, or school schedules, and holiday plans. Occasionally, they might slip into discussing more meaningful topics like happiness and health.

'Are you happy now?'

'Now? As in right at this moment? Yes.'

'Thank you but no, I meant – are you on top of things ...?'

But she wouldn't let him finish, getting on top of 'things' to waylay him from that line of questioning. And as determined a man as Bibek was, he could not persist in grilling her about her happiness when she was making *him* so happy. It would seem churlish to keep on talking. Five minutes later, she'd swallowed and they could talk again, this time about common friends in Kolkata from whence they hailed.

'You heard about Gugloo and Babli? Eeesh!'

'Shorbonash! Everyone knows about this now?'

'I am not everyone.'

'No, you certainly are not.'

Yet, they never did talk about love. Love had been discussed long ago and lost in the mists of time. The discussion of love, that is. Its reality still clung to them or they wouldn't have found themselves in that dark little room again, with limbs entangled, speaking of their affection softly, even if the words they used were 'fish', 'books', and sometimes, 'rosogolla'. And if passion was not parsed, there was no frenzied furrowing into each other either. It was almost as if they were working, albeit languidly, towards the lying in each other's arms after. Raima thought about the old married couples she'd heard of who did that, even as she congratulated herself on *her* marriage having more heat.

When the burst of conversation about mutual friends and interests subsided, they listened to the noises outside the window, drifting in and out of sleep. The sound of feet and cars trundling past, mingled with their gentle snores and occasional nuzzling. Of course, there's only so much time busy adults with children can devote to such indulgences, and they un-undressed in unison, as people used to each other do, after an hour of their dreamy half-doze. Clothes had neither been torn off, nor would be flung on. It would all be at the same placid pace as their lovemaking, because they weren't heading anywhere. Nowhere new. Dinner, too, would be at one of their favourite joints, discovered over the years to hit just the right spot, before Raima journeyed on. As she always did.

'Food?' she pressed.

'Must you leave right after?' Bibek grumbled mildly. He didn't really mind; he had other 'little things' (in his words) lined up.

'Such a lot of work tomorrow,' she said evasively, and they both knew she lied. 'Let's go to the steakhouse though,' Raima carried on brightly, a sop to him for her planned desertion later, because of course, she really preferred fish.

Linking arms with the ease of long-time lovers, they strolled down to the hotel lobby where they approached the receptionist, without any of that shifty-eyed skulking that often attend illicit new couplings. The newer and more taboo, the more shifty and breathless usually, like the couple nervously waiting for their keys in the corner. Raima spotted them and was immediately absorbed in what she imagined was their tale of duplicity and longing, leaving Bibek to discuss the room with reception. While that was none of her concern, these two most certainly were! She felt it her duty to earwig; who knew what life lessons might emerge?

'So,' the man with the sharp bones of an anxious Russian hitman was saying, 'you like living in Bristol?'

'Yes,' said the bespectacled black girl quietly, 'it's fresh and fun, and well, you can do whatever you want.' Raima thought she bit back the 'like right now', but then the girl continued, 'How I miss the ladies' fingers!'

'Huh?' said the craggy-cheeked man. On his face was a look of alarm that was more than the uneasy stasis of the illegal (Raima surmised) immigrant. Had he picked up a lesbian by mistake, he seemed to wonder. Could his strong, square fingers possibly match a woman's for nimbleness? Should he risk it at all?

Whether she cottoned on or not, his lover-to-be kept a straight face, 'Okra. I miss my mom's okra and black-eyed peas. They live in Yorkshire now but still cook Jamaican. Thank god! The jerk though, I don't have to miss. Plenty here.'

'Not this one,' her Russian friend cracked a smile for the first time.

Raima looked at him with more interest. He was catching on to the girl's patter fast. No longer panicked but playing along, he seemed less of the skinhead she had thought at first. She was getting a good feeling about them; that they might take it beyond this brief encounter, this unlikely couple. She watched with pleasure their otherness from each other. And from her and her man. Not only in how they 'accidentally' brushed against each other with trepidation and yearning, but what diametric opposites they were in appearance. The girl was dark and softly rounded with a cascade of braids running down her back, while he was all angles, stubble (even on his pate) and ghostly pallor. While she and her partner, why, they could be brother and sister. No one would question *their* couplehood because they looked so like society dictated a couple should look. Both brown-skinned, small and bespectacled, with a similar upbringing and memories of the past, it was like looking in the mirror, Raima reflected, with the same rush of warmth for a familiar, comforting image. But frenzied passion was harder to arouse for your own image in the mirror. How narcissistic would that be?

Bibek finished talking to reception and turned to leave. With Raima, who had been inching towards the door since the younger couple lapsed into silence and grew less intriguing, catching up quickly. They held hands tightly now as their time together dwindled. Yet, as they walked out into the luminous evening, Raima regaling Bibek with the derring-do of the other duo, they were nattering as nonchalantly as they'd been naked earlier. Dinner in a little bistro they'd visited before, which specialised in hearty meat dishes, was a comfortable affair as well. He dived into his sizzling ribeye and roast potatoes with as much satisfaction as he had displayed in bed the hour before. Knowing him like she did, Raima wasn't put out by that at all, but the blandness of her own tucked-away-on-the-menu trout in wilting spinach order chafed, and so she said the only thing that sprang to her mind at that moment to spice up dinner. Raima brought up the other man.

'Really?' Bibek asked, wonderstruck, more envious of cooking skills he didn't possess than the time she spent with the competition. 'He cooks every day? And *every* day it's fabulous?'

'Oh yes!' Raima affirmed, turning her attention back to her suddenly more scrumptious fish, pleased to have stirred him even a little. He retorted irritably that she 'manufactured pinpricks', but their battle went no further. Because it was almost time for her to go. Bolting down a shared dessert of a walnut brownie with green tea ice cream (she got the brownie; he, the oddly matched ice cream), they strolled to the platform from where her train would depart. If they weren't arm-in-arm as before, it had nothing to do with their only run-in of the night, and everything with the fact that both had already moved on in their thoughts to what the future held. Consequently, their goodbye at the stiles was neither long nor lingering, but a quick affectionate peck planted distractedly.

Watching him go, Raima boards her train with a skip in her step, her every thought now fixed on journey's end. Sliding into her seat, she feels a new woman. Not that she isn't happy with who she was minutes before, but that has run its course. She fixes her short, layered hair looking into the darkened window. Then checks her uneven, guaranteed-to-snag-spinach teeth in the little silver mirror she draws out from her handbag, and is relieved to find none. With a little shiver of excitement next, she dives into her bag to fish out the keys she's secreted in it. The keys Neil had handed her when she'd left the previous morning, neither of them ever sure that she would return. But now she holds them up triumphantly and tightly, like you would a talisman, as the train takes her back. As much as she loves Bibek, she never feels this exhilaration on her way to him as she does coming back. Where Bibek warmed, Neil ignites. Yet, she's not actually comparing them because she has headspace merely for one and can only think ahead. It's a late train and she's alone in her carriage, except for the old man sleeping with his head bouncing uncomfortably against the window. Raima decides it would be safe to throw her own head back against the slippery seat, and with her eyes closed, press her thighs together, rubbing away the kisses planted betwixt just hours before, readying them for more. She sucks urgently on a mint as the train heads into the darkened station of her destination and her excitement mounts. And then she's there.

The cabbie at the station entrance nods reassuringly as they head off into the colder night of the north. Despite the chill, Raima winds her window down to air her clothes out of the smells of dinner (and just maybe of another man). There is no need, however, to air out her head; it is focused on Future Man and, as a result, giddy with happiness. The cabbie jumps slightly when she breaks into song but isn't seriously surprised. He has taken her to her destination before, usually at odd hours, and always singing! Raima's lovelorn song in her youthful voice has no basis in fact, however. Having said her tender goodbyes to Bibek over dinner (with words like 'banana' and 'books' again), she has no recollection of him. Or the cabbie who has driven her back before. Luckily, he remembers the way to her stop better than she does.

'Here we are, Didi,' he says, as he always does, with his broad Bangladeshi smile.

They've stopped in front of a roomy, red brick house, and Raima approaches the lit-up front door eagerly, fumbling with the talismanic keys. Once inside the darkened hallway though, she's ever so quiet – it's long after bedtime and she plans to tiptoe her way up to the bedroom in which Neil sleeps. The stairs creak as she climbs, despite her best efforts at avoiding the spots she knows are noisy. Slowly swinging the unlocked door open, she sees him sleeping on his side in the king-sized bed, moonlight streaming in through the sash windows to bathe him in a pearly light. His pale hair glows and the muscles on his lean frame are silvered. They are bunched in anticipation and she knows he's only half-asleep, lying in wait for her. Not unlike how pleasurably on edge she'd been through her journey. All in all, Raima thinks greedily, he makes a delectable picture.

Dropping her clothes at the foot of the bed, she gets between the sheets and spoons him till he stirs. Her breasts pressing into his back can still wake him and he turns towards her. No, he pounces and she is dragged under him, fighting for breath but giggling with pleasure. She attempts to stifle them, because they mustn't rouse the house. But he's not finished, pushing her legs apart demandingly and finding his way in, even as his mouth locks into hers. There is no talk of fish, friends and family now, this is visceral and hungry and grasping. In fact, there is no talk. There is grinding, gasping and groans. The weight of him is almost painful, as are the forceful thrusts, but she loves this rough and tumble. This sex with teeth and talons, scraping, biting, grazing, even as they move with a furious tempo towards their mutual climax. This is what she came back for – this is what she always comes back for – as sore as it might leave her, with a creeping yearning for the comfort of Bibek. But that last feeling disappears as they reach their thigh-clenching, lip-biting crescendo, with the even more pleasurable prospect of the little ones on the morrow.

'So glad you're back,' he says as he turns over, silvery in the moonlight again, and tranquil this time. Nothing else had been said, or will be, till the morning.

They sleep a long, deep sleep. Here, there are no noises from the street outside. There is barely a street, the house half-hidden in the trees. The sky pales and still they sleep. Until the room floods with light, all of a sudden. It isn't a sudden break in the lowering clouds that had welcomed Raima last night, but caramel children loping in, as bright-eyed and bushy-tailed as every morning, pushing doors wide open and drapes aside. They scramble in between Raima and Neil, unconcerned that they are naked, not surprised by the churned sheets, the scratched skin on their parents. 'Did you get hot in the night from making all that noise, Mommy, and have to take your clothes off?' asked the seven-year-old with a sly smile that said she was growing up. And anyway, Mommy had worse wounds on her wrists often. The younger ones rain kisses on Raima, only glad she'd returned. There was always a tiny kernel of worry in their minds that she wouldn't, but she was back and awake and smiling at her babies, and nothing else mattered. Their arms tighten around her hot and firm, and she responds with a comforting clinch that encircles all three. Then the youngest pipes up, his brow crinkling,

'Mommy left her little things behind again.' Raima looks over from those in her arms to her bedside table. Standing atop are the littlest big things in her life, her tiny, green, life-impeding Schizophrenia pills that she leaves behind ever so often. Just so she can *be*.

BEYONCÉ AND JAY-JI

'See now,' he said to the jowly policeman opposite, 'you let me out of here and I can get you all sorts of bishbosh. The freshest puppies on this side of Tiptop.' That was before he made a V with his middle and index finger and pointed downwards towards his groin. The policeman was shocked. Was this the confession then? And if it was, how was he meant to record this twaddle? This was a middle-aged man, and yet he didn't make any sense. It strengthened his belief in the man's guilt. 'Why do you talk like that?' he asked, narrowing his rheumy blue eyes. The man, slouching across the table from him, looked a bit shamefaced then. He was portly, bald and bespectacled. Like he might be a software engineer on a slow crawl to retirement. And maybe a closet poet. Not like a man who would wear a baseball cap backwards, pants that pooled around his lower legs, and speak in that ridiculous patois. 'Just got used to it,' the man

mumbled, 'easier to grab a kid if you know his tongue.'
My god, thought the policeman with eyes popping from
excitement, here it comes – the admission they'd been
waiting half a day for. Perhaps even in language they
understood. The other three cops hiding behind the two-
way mirror had already started counting their chickens.
How many pieces precisely in each bucket they would
order from KFC once they'd got this MF slammed up.

When the man opened his mouth again, the veteran
cop got so excited he looked close to climax. The other
three leaned so far in that they might have fallen through
the mirror had it been less solid. 'I just wanted to be their
Poop Dawg, y'know.' The officers stared at each other. Did
he really say Poop Dog? It certainly sounded like he did,
and it didn't sound good. Maybe they didn't 'git his lingo'
but they knew a scumbag when they saw one. A brown
man dressed like a black man, calling himself Jay-ji, FFS.
'Cause I've got Beyoncé, innit,' he'd explained, chortling
at his own joke (which was greeted with pin-drop silence
from the police). His file said he was a Jayant Kumar, and
they knew these brown feckers called each other Ji, though
they hadn't a clue why. Some kind of lowlife code maybe.
'Wasn't doing it for me though,' the man continued
plaintively. 'Those kids have been gagging for it,' he
insisted, mystified by his interrogator's electrified reaction.
The plainclothes man questioning him went purple and
gripped the table edge to stop himself from reaching for
the suspect. Was that excitement, Jay-ji wondered a trifle
doubtfully. Did the police guy want to gather him in an

ecstatic embrace? At any rate, he decided to take the officer's reaction as a good sign. Were there deals to be made here? Might they want a piece of the action too? 'They wanted a lot of Babazook, y'know, and some Honeybuns. And those amazing Shadrocks from Doopladipdob.' 'They couldn't get enough, in fact,' he continued happily, 'so I took them to quiet corners to give them the full Phitphat.' The lady standing in the shadows at the back of the room took a few steps forward then. 'My god, YOU sick man! These are children you're talking about. I don't for a minute believe they wanted any of your ... flipflops,' she finished, looking flustered.

'But they do!' exclaimed the man with glee. 'These seventeen-year-olds want what all seventeen-year-olds want. What they can't have in these parts. This little town here wraps you in soundproof cotton wool, cutting you off from the outside world. But they yearn for a taste of that world; the Crockswop that's all the rage in the big cities. And they'll have a bit of that Taptitumtap too if they can. Sweeeet I tell you. Works out so well for me.' The lady social worker was shaking in the meantime at the man's barefaced perversion, while the policeman was oscillating wildly between exultation and bewilderment. He'd got a full confession. Yet, what had the man confessed to? 'Or I would've given them a gutful of what they desired, if you gupshups hadn't come blundering in. I was told it was a quiet spot. I had them all lined up, ready for the hurbydurby, and then what happens? You lot cause havoc. Not even stopping to ask nicely for my swag!'

And so it continued over the next hours, the suspect spilling the beans and the police gathering them fastidiously, even if they couldn't tell the mungo from the runner. Either way, this man wouldn't be allowed to *do* a runner, with the police stitching his case tightly shut.

All this, while the other team led by Inspector Hotpot worked on getting the children's side of the story. But they weren't making much headway either. That morning, standing outside yet another family's ostentatious front door, waiting for them to let her capacious frame in, Hotpot of the Worsham Woods Police was reflecting on the fact that she'd had many, many successes in her policing career, but this was not going to be one of them. She fixed the elephant-headed knocker with a baleful glare. They had planned the operation perfectly. They had heard of the clandestine meetings in the carpark between this Jay-ji and the teenagers from the village school. It was the oldest batch and they often stayed after classes. Thus, the hardest to protect but still children, and so when the news broke of their being lured to the carpark, their parents and the school and, indeed, the police, went into a frenzy. The man had been watched closely for weeks, and on that fateful night with the smell of a storm in the air, he was caught red-handed. With his hands down his pants to be precise, rummaging, for god's sake, while a ring of riveted children stood around him. An exhibitionist as well as a paedo, Hotpot thought with some satisfaction. He was lucky all they found in his car were stacks and stacks of the most abominable music that the officers had ever heard (they didn't listen for too long; only as much as they needed to know it was irrelevant). Neither incriminating photos nor drugs were found in Jay-ji's car or on his person, to the dismay of the police for whom these were the twin pillars of conviction in the murkier cases. It should have been an open-and-shut case as a matter of fact, but now, gathering the testimony of the kids, she could see it was destined to be messy.

She didn't like kids, of course, and that didn't help because they always cottoned on. Despite that, the police force insisted on putting her on 'domestic' cases because she was a woman. She hated that she would have to handle these gangling teenagers with kid gloves. What they needed was to be shaken up a bit, mock press-ganged into telling the police what they knew. She sighed. That wasn't going to happen; not in a sensitive investigation like this. Not in a comfortable suburb, and with puffed-up parents like theirs. She'd had to instruct her team to tenderly tut and tip-toe, treating the children like the treasures their folks thought they were. This was the directive from on high. And she had to feign agreement as best as she could. So, here she was again at one of their nice homes, and this time she had been saddled with that bleeding-heart social worker she liked even less than the kids. This was the woman behind all the mollycoddling and pussyfooting their team was forced to do. Now with the door finally open to them, she was being allowed to pussyfoot her way up the stairs to gently coax the teens into revealing what they knew. She fought to keep the rictus-like smile pasted on her face.

'I don't remember,' the oldest boy said blankly, in response to her first question about the events of that night.

'But we actually brought you home from that parking lot right after we apprehended the culprit, so you must remember that you were there? And if you can recall that, surely you remember what you did there?'

The boy looked uncomfortable, and she yearned to give him a little clout on the head to help him recall. Having spoken to most of the kids present that night (barring the one girl who'd claimed illness and stayed away from this meeting; that would be another trek they'd have to make, huffed Hotpot), they were no wiser. The kids were clearly frightened though; they kept muttering under their breath about 'bundybashers' or 'mampydoodles', and most worryingly, 'go-blows'. Or, at least, that's all the police could make out. Gobbledygook again, like the man Jay-ji's breathless patter. They all kept surreptitiously sliding sidelong glances at each other too, and most of all at the boy called Harry (or Hari, if you were his recently relocated Grandmother).

Harry, who was patently leader of this pack. Harry, who was trying very hard to hang on to his cool, but failing so badly even his crew had begun to notice. Harry, whose existential crisis had led to their twilit treks into the deserted carpark in the first place. Harry, who was trying to fill that hole that had opened up in his life when he crossed the threshold of childhood into not-quite-adult-ness. What had he filled it with, was the question all the adults watching this unfolding drama were asking. What troubles had he led his tribe into?

Of course, Harry knew. But how could he reveal to his demanding family who he really was deep down inside his perfect son exterior? How would his doting parents cope with his preference for Bumbadil to the everyday foofah they'd hoped he'd take to and make them proud? No, he couldn't tell them what he was actually doing there that night, so he said, 'I was just crossing the parking lot to go home. That's when I saw a figure hanging about in the half-dark and went to investigate.' Harry made sure he didn't make eye contact with anyone while speaking. When Bali, the youngest at fifteen and three quarters, was questioned, he followed suit, used as he was to mirroring Harry. Soon they were all looking furtive and the police knew they were on to something. The fuzz knew things had been going off in that carpark a while. There may well have been other kids before this batch. But they got there in time to catch the miscreants for the very first time that night. So, there were kids to question for a change, and things to find out. They found out, for example, that a few of them were 'getting the goods' for the first time that night. That this hadn't 'come off' as planned (which made all the grown-ups feel so much better, they almost stopped digging further). And that meetings were arranged with Jay-ji only when the children craved more 'squish'. They shuddered at the thought of the squish, hardened police officers though they were. But they had enough to nail their man. They wouldn't need to talk to the absent girl at all now.

Absent too was any physical evidence that the kids had been harmed. There were no easily spotted bruises or the usual physical signs of abuse. Their families had also balked at the idea of their being examined in any invasive way. The police too had backed off, knowing that in well-heeled suburban cases like theirs, it was the families who decided how far the investigation would go. They were, however, as convinced as the police that Jay-ji had undue influence on their kids. Perhaps he was the guru of a cult. Why else did they all speak the same Satanic tongue? And meet in dark places? Why else had they been standing around him in a ritual circle while he did unspeakable things in front of them? It was a cult, they were sure, but they also convinced themselves that no assault had taken place and no doctors need get involved. Their children were still pure.

Jay-ji liked them pure too, he ruminated sitting in the station cell. He liked to bring them over to his way of thinking. It was the thrill of the chase he liked more than the actual transaction. Then again, he reflected, that little exchange of the precious stuff also made him smile for days. And the kids, they smiled too. He had seen them walking around school with smirks they hugged to themselves like their new secrets. He should perhaps not have been watching, but he took pride in having introduced them to wonders new. Because he gave them pure gold. He kept his stash in his pimped-up car and when he brought it out, the kids were dazzled every time. Gosh, he had stuff like no one else in their small town. Twenty years ago, he had started with Beyoncé, but she'd grown old and now he had Maze and Haze and Hoohah. He liked how fresh they were and the newness of it all blew the kids' minds. That's what kept them coming back for more. They came back because he gave them experiences they couldn't get anywhere else. They called it 'squish'. And sure, they liked pulling the wool over their parents' eyes too. And hey, he soliloquized, mentally patting himself on the back, he never took much from them in return; nothing they weren't ready to part with.

So he couldn't understand why the police, the parents, the courts were now so eager to see him as a monster. It baffled him. He explained his modus operandi to them again and again to make them understand the simple joyful equation between him and his young 'posse'. Sometimes, he held forth with relish because he was proud of how he eased these awkward children into becoming the coolest, most grown-up in town. What he was, as he saw it, was a conduit. A source of things mind-blowingly new. He reeled off the names of some of his 'collaborators' now for the police. Turk, Bo-Zo, Blimp-Three-Four-Five. The police looked at him aghast but also eager. Why was he so pleased to be turning his henchmen over? What kind of simpleton was he? Or, or could he be the cunning, evil monster they'd first figured he was, hoodwinking them in ways they didn't realise? Was it possible to be both? And imagine the coup it would be when they caught all these criminals, and oh, the promotions across the board for the police!

It just so happened that in the pursuit of these slimiest of pervs from around the country, their intelligence wing (to the extent that you can call Larry, sitting in a twilit booth off reception because there was no other room for him, their 'intelligence') discovered something disturbing. All the names of the paedos that Jay-ji had coughed up seemed to correspond with those of brand new – so new they were barely hatched – bleeding-edge musicians from across the country. Rarely white or from the right side of the tracks, these were the performers parents wouldn't want their children listening to. Did paedos appropriate the cool names of bonafide musicians as cover? Or were the latter in fact as deeply dodgy as the police of Worsham Woods had always suspected? Notice, they remarked to each other, how none of them looked remotely respectable; horrific masses of head-to-toe tattoos no doubt hidden by their dark skin colour.

Inspector Hotpot sighed again. Hadn't all the rigmarole from both their principal culprit as well as his victims been bad enough without this confusion? They remembered the stacks of obscure, almost alien music they'd found in Jay-ji's car which they had ignored as unimportant. It was Larry's job now to sift through it all. Would he find the most heinous crimes recorded on them? Could he bear to listen? Would it turn his stomach? Instead, the next day, Loz was found eagerly scuttling into his little cubicle, putting his headphones on and rocking away, back and forth in his chair for hours, looking all shook up but not in the way they'd expected. His colleagues were concerned they had somehow allowed him to slip under the influence of this strange cult they had unearthed. A cult of coloured, cutting-edge songsters. Or 'squish'.

It was at this time that the children appeared to have been galvanised into action too. Meeting at Harry's house, they had decided they wouldn't be able to live with themselves if they didn't come clean. They wouldn't, in fact, feel clean again unless they owned up to their entirely voluntary grubby activities. Activities that had indeed involved clandestine meetings with the unsavoury Jay-ji. In dark, deserted places. It had unfortunately entailed squeezing into his greasy car in a tangle of sweaty limbs (pimped-up it may've been on the outside, it smelled of butter chicken within). They were indeed guilty of holding their breath while he brought out his wares, and then taking the plunge. Most of all, they knew the little secrets they came away with, tucked into their pants, hidden in their clothes, were wrong. Distasteful. Even illegal. Had they been hanging out at the dime store and nicking the odd track, they would have been less in the wrong than getting stuff so new it hadn't hit the market. That, after all, was why they had to go to juddering old Jay-ji with their strange new tastes. Only he could supply what they wanted: more Haze, Maze, Hoohah, Bumbadil and Dipplydoo than anyone else for miles around. He was the local purveyor of radical new music, sourced illegally and sold to the kids cheap. They needed to come clean, they needed to confess to their sins and clear Jay-ji of those pinned on him. But most of all, they needed to keep getting their hands on that heady, giddy, earth-shaking squish.

'Huh?' barked the policeman who'd originally interrogated old Jay, almost apoplectic. 'So, he's been slipping you songs and not body parts? He lured you into dingy carparks to ply you with music, not drugs, and NOT sex?' The youngest of the children looked at the policeman horrified that he had said the S word. Hadn't the same man lectured them two weeks ago about avoiding pervs? The kids had never imagined *that* was why everyone was making such a fuss. The very utterance of the scary word, however, caused a seismic shift in the room. The focus of everyone's distaste shifted to their bungling police force that had handled the case so badly. The parents announced that they were dropping charges. They would communicate that to the missing family too, that of the girl who'd been sick since the incident. They were confident the latter would go along happily. Back to being perfect, untampered families, they felt bad about having put the misunderstood man through the rigours of arrest and incarceration, even though they didn't like his clothes, his taste in music, or the fact that he was taking money, however small (since they hadn't noticed any missing), off their kids. They wondered if they should invite the unfortunate fellow to dinner. They had heard he had once been one of them, with a picket-fenced home and a white-collar job in IT. His wife had left him apparently, taking their children with her in an acrimonious split, and it had all fallen apart for him. Perhaps if they embraced him to the bosom of good society again, he might cease and desist from his minor crimes (and the major disruption he'd caused with them this time). Inspector Hotpot was eager to be rid of them all now that the veneer of conviviality had been blown, so she quickly agreed to each of their demands as she saw them out.

The kids convened later that evening. A little celebration for a crisis sorted. No, a biggish celebration considering even their absent friend had turned up, though she didn't look very well at all. But there was more than one reason to celebrate, and they were glad to have got together after the long weekend of worry and confusion. Their supplier was out of the slammer and it would be business as usual for the contraband-hungry kids. Except that Harry had a plan, a plan from which they could profit from the scudding cloud that had cast a temporary shadow on Jay-ji. A plan that would make the most of their heroic rescue of their old mucker in the nick of time, without which he'd be on his way to prison now. 'He'd be grateful, right?' asked Harry, but only rhetorically. 'Now that we've had him set free, maybe he'll give us a few for free, eh?' They all laughed at the idea of giving the dealer a taste of his own medicine, doing him out of a quid or two. He'd never charged much, but why pay anything at all if they could help it? It would be a 'welcome home' prank on their completely harmless, rather pathetic, but really quite lovely old pal.

Only then did the girl who'd stayed out of everything speak up. 'But,' she cleared her throat. The others rolled their eyes. She'd always been the softest touch and they weren't going to let her argue them out of their happy little jape with any plea for clemency on the old man's behalf. 'But,' she said again in a tiny whisper, 'it was never money he took from me.'

THE MEMORY PROJECT

'She looked like a tree sprite, a shankchunni, but a very pretty one, standing silent and half-smiling under the spreading branches of our old mango tree,' Deep was saying, his face animated with the memory of that summer long ago. 'She came to us the year you started that venture with the weavers, remember?' But his mother was clearly only half-listening, her attention pinned on the simmering pot of hybrid rice and shrimp she called khichotto ('When khichdi meets risotto,' she would laugh), which she was seasoning and stirring in turn. Perhaps a dash too much salt had already gone into it because his father appeared suddenly alarmed, looking up from the newspaper from which he rarely surfaced. But when his wife continued to give more importance to her swill than her son, he, too, settled back into his comfy chair and got on with his reading. Deep prattled on, this benign disinterest from his parents so familiar, that it was comforting. 'I first saw her from the shadow of the porch where I was playing, but when she looked over, I knew I'd been spotted and trotted up. She watched me as I walked up, like a cat, I thought. As carefully as I had been observing her.'

To his grandiose seven-year-old wave and huge gap-toothed smile, she smiled back slightly and tipped her head in welcome (that had made him giggle even then; wasn't this *his* house, his mango tree?). Or maybe it was to see him better (she wore big glasses, after all, like his mother). But for the most part, she seemed to stand stock-still and as quiet as the tree branching out over her. 'Are you here for me?' he had asked her. She'd thought this over a good long while before she agreed that she was, tilting her head farther forward (Deep could recall being terribly impressed as, to his knowledge, only Nearly Headless Nick could do that!). Back then, the time she took to mull it over also worked like a character certificate. 'Because at seven,' he recalled, 'I gave as much thought to every question, whether they were about my aspirations when I grew up – it was an explorer I wanted to be that year, I'm sure – to how much jam I needed slathered on my toast. It showed me she took me seriously.'

Deep did not, however, take his parental distraction to mean *they* didn't take him seriously. He was happy to hold forth uninterrupted on the work he had before him. Having his parents as mostly silent sounding boards had always helped him gather and firm up his ideas, as it was doing now. He was hoping to produce something quite special, even startling, for his university writing project.

The 'Memory Project' it had been dubbed by his class, as it involved digging deep into their subconscious and coming up with stories from their own lives, yet distant enough, in terms of time or ties, to make the process more demanding than an everyday spot of scribbling. 'That's nice, dear,' his mother offered distractedly, as she sniffed the pot for missing ingredients ('The Nose knows,' his father liked to joke when she did this), and added her third round of Tabasco. She could have meant the story he was narrating, or that she was pleased the woman looking after him in her absence had taken him seriously. Yet, did that slight furrow on her brow indicate worry? That she had over-spiced her culinary concoction, or under-listened to her flesh-and-blood creation?

Deep continued, 'When she spoke for the first time, she had the quietest, most faraway voice. Like the wind rushing through long grass.' At that, his father stirred, and looked nostalgic, all of a sudden. Deep fervently hoped he was not about to embark (like all dads do) on a highly coloured story of some imagined derring-do in his misspent youth. Instead, he cleared his throat and asked, 'What, er, did she say?' 'Oh, nothing much,' Deep replied, amused by his father's unexpected interest in an incident from his childhood. 'But don't you recall you were there, Baba? Just as she started speaking for the first time, saying something so soft (but rather melodious) that I could barely catch, I saw you come outside and look over at us. And then you jumped a little. I remember that because it was so unlike you!' His father's much older avatar jumped a little too, in his seat. It was more like a squirm and Deep put it down to his riveting telling of the story. If his father, of all people, was responding to it, then he must have managed to inject the right amount of atmosphere. 'I don't remember this, I have to admit,' his father mumbled.

'I'm not surprised, Baba! I barely remembered it myself till I started digging deep,' Deep said, chuckling at his own joke (he had a lot of his father in him after all). 'But I do recall now that you came out just as she'd begun talking, asking me questions about myself in her faint, faraway voice. You had stopped and looked at us a good while, too, and then you must have decided I was in safe hands, because you turned back into the house, the shadows swallowing you conclusively.' His mother dropped her brass ladle with a clang and looked at her husband in bafflement. On the counter, the soupy mix she'd been stirring into her rice was evaporating as quickly as her own enthusiasm for cooking that day. She seemed as though she was about to speak when his father climbed into the breach with an agility he hadn't shown in years. 'There were workmen in our house, too, that day, remember, Paro? I would have gone back in to oversee that damp wall they were repairing. This house, Deep,' he said, swivelling towards his son, turning his back on the stony silence that was leaning over the stove, fishing out the cinnamon sticks that should never have gone in at all, 'is two hundred years old, as you know. There's so much we don't know about it. But the workmen thought there was something behind the damp wall that was causing the damage, and I was eager to see it. With you occupied, I knew I could.'

Deep saw his mother relax a little. Their house had indeed had work done on it that summer. 'It's funny that you should mention the house, because that's exactly what my new friend wanted to see. She watched you go back in with a surprising intentness, and then, with her delicate face close to my ear, she whispered that she loved the look of our house. How she'd loved to live in a house like ours! I was surprised because I thought she did. That she was nanny to the England-returned kid next door who could only speak English. I was taken enough with her to readily agree to show her around ours.

'When I took her hand to guide her in, it was surprisingly cool to the touch. I noticed also how light her tread was, as if she were gliding, where I was stomping in my seven-year-old style. Everything about her was feathery, wispy, light.' Yet, as he waxed lyrical about her, he could see his mother's troubled face. Worried, no doubt, that the khichotto was not going to plan. The pot was smoking like nothing other than a charcuterie should, and a burnt smell was emanating from its depths, reminding the two men of the time her roast chicken had exploded spectacularly in their faces. To avoid further explosions, Deep reassured his mother, 'Actually, she looked a lot like you. Familiar. A face I could trust. But a paler copy.' He had bitten back the word 'ethereal' just in time. His mother laughed at this turnaround Deep had so adroitly managed. Like father, like son, she thought wryly.

All those years ago, once his father had disappeared into the back of the house, where the workmen were clanging, banging and breaking through the wall, the two of them, little boy and gossamer girl, had crept up the stairs. The surreptitious nature of this, like some secret mission, had excited the imaginative child that he was. And as his father had as much as given them his approval, he had nothing to worry about. Pushing aside his mother's warning voice in his head, he had led his visitor to the landing. The bedrooms stood clustered around it, facing each other, as in all the colonial homes of that period. And by the side of the bathroom was a wrought-iron staircase leading further up. 'I wanted to show her my bedroom because it was a new possession and I was tremendously proud of it. I had just been moved out of the anteroom to your big bedroom, remember? Into a full-fledged room of my own. This was freshly painted in the sky blue I had asked for, and all my prized possessions had been neatly arranged on shelves around the room the week before. As I excitedly talked her through all my treasures, poor, patient woman, she gravitated towards the window that overlooked the courtyard with the tree.'

'This is such a lovely house, isn't it?' she reflected then, rather than asked. 'It almost wouldn't matter who you were here with, would it?' He hadn't known how to respond, but for the first time, he sensed there was more to her than her pale pretty face and light poplin blouse. 'I like living here with Ma and Baba,' he offered hesitantly.

But she was already on her way out of his bedroom and into his parents'.

She walked straight to the dressing table and started moving the framed photos around. Little Deep walked up to stand beside her. 'You look like my mom,' Deep suggested, struck by how very similar they were, as he looked from her photo to the young woman beside him. 'No,' she shook her head, as if slightly put out, 'look at this though.' She held up an old silver filigree frame he had ignored all his life because the picture was too faded to appeal to him. *And* it was of old people he'd never known. 'We *all* look like her,' she said, tilting her head again in that characteristic gesture towards the gaggle of young girls in the photo, at the centre of which was, Deep scrunched up his face to try and remember, his great-grandmother in her youth. But before he could ask questions, she had set down the frame and moved on. Suddenly, all that stillness and quiet was replaced with fire and haste. She was running towards the wrought-iron stairs and was up them in a trice. Deep scrambled after, the reassuring sounds of the workmen, with his dad amongst them, falling away as they entered the dark attic.

In the room at the back of the house, something surreal was taking shape too, as the workmen removed more and more of the damp-stained modern wall to find a hollow behind it. A twilit hollow which smelt of all their yesterdays; the scent of old paper, slowly and almost pleasantly rotting wood, mixed not unexpectedly with the whiff of damp undergrowth, but also, astonishingly, the fragrance of scented garments. His father volunteered this information quickly, almost as if he wished to head his wife off at the pass. Or to distract her with a pleasant mystery to counteract the effect of Deep's unsettling story. It was certainly not the waywardness of her second wave of ingredients; the pepper, Thai fish sauce and garlic pods, and their failure to shape up into the dish she wanted to cook, that was upsetting her. Most of all, his father clearly hoped to exonerate himself, 'I wasn't far away. Just in the back room where the wall had finally fallen and the men gone silent. We were silent because we were stunned by what we saw. A room beyond the damp wall, but no ordinary room ...'

'Hush!' said his mother, obviously incensed. 'If you didn't tell me about it then, you don't need to now!' Then, turning her attention and some of her fury on her son, even as she swirled the khichotto around till it bubbled like Mt Vesuvius, 'And you? What happened to you? How often had I told you to be careful ...?' With his mother in a militant mood, waving her ladle around, and with pots of boiling food and kitchen knives at the ready, attempting a hug would have been injudicious, but Deep rushed in to comfort with words. 'You know how we are without you, Ma. While Baba was losing a part of the house, I was losing my way in it. The girl had a strange effect on me from the moment I met her – part Mary Poppins and partly you – I found myself willing to go wherever she led.'

'In the attic,' he carried on with his story while he had his mother's attention (he had his father's, too, but the poor man was no longer feeling brave enough to emerge from behind his newspaper), 'though it was pitch-dark, she moved around more surefootedly than anywhere else in the house. She paced at first, and thought aloud, still apparently unsettled by the pictures in your bedroom. Or perhaps the bedroom itself, which she had left quickly.' 'Burgundy shutters aren't to everyone's taste,' his father now murmured, risking his life.

'Can we go back down please, miss?' Deep had asked softly. It was *his* loud, naughty voice that was disappearing into nothingness, the first pinpricks of fear drying up his throat, while hers gained power as it swelled into a rant on cosy couples in great houses. In the midst of her diatribe, she had stopped to fiddle with the skylight. 'This opens,' she insisted, glowering at the little boy, as if it was his fault the pane wouldn't shift, 'but you need to be taller.' Yet, she had, in the process of struggling with it, let in a tiny glimmer. And in that light, the wispy young woman was taking on a new dimension. She looked distinctly larger, Deep worried, as if the darkness had fed her to twice her size. Walking to the farthest end of the room, she sat down unerringly on the little bed hidden in the eaves. That bed which had not been used since his mother was a child in this house, sleeping in it when aunts stayed over. He had expected a big puff of dust to come off it when she sat down. But none did.

'Well, the house was all topsy-turvy with the workmen in, Paro ...'

'Are you seriously suggesting they'd been lying down in the attic in between bouts of wall-breaking?'

Deep was amazed that instead of cowering in the face of his mother's rage – rage that had nothing to do with her khichotto burning to a crisp while she turned on one man and then another with anger – his father ploughed on, 'But what we found amazed us to such a degree, we lost sight of everything else. Beyond the wall was a room. But more like a nest. A human nest. Built by nature and by hand, lovingly. Bricks, branches, naturally unkempt undergrowth – all had been harnessed and twisted and turned till it formed a large, earthy cocoon. Inside, there were lanterns hung but snuffed out a while ago. There was moss and leaves matting the rounded, chrysalid walls. But they had been warped and twined into braids. With loops of dried flowers running through them. And in the centre – heaps of sheets, floral sheets, as if stolen from washing lines up and down the neighbourhood! A bed for a young woman ...'

At which he stopped and looked nervous as his wife appeared more thunderous, still. Deep took the opportunity to pick up where he'd left off. 'From her perch on the bed, she beckoned me over in a gruff voice. Seriously, Ma, a growly voice,' he directed a tiny smile at his mother to cheer her up, which it didn't, of course. Even the most beguiling smile from her beloved son would not calm her, mid-stream into stories that shook her world. But having come this far, he now had to tell her everything. 'It may have been more of a hiss, actually. And she herself seemed to wax and wane in size, shape-shifting with the shadows. I was seriously frightened by then, so much so, my leaden legs wouldn't move. When I turned to flee, I stumbled. She must have moved quickly, because she was towering over me before I could get up. Reaching down to grab me. That's when we heard a gigantic crash from downstairs!'

The lid from the pot decided to do an encore at just that moment. Blown off by the steam gathering under, it clattered to the floor at his father's feet. As if his mother was saying, 'Look what you've done,' without even moving a muscle. She stood as still as a statue. Or the people of Pompei, petrified for posterity in the ashes of their ignorance. But Deep knew her well enough to know it was only the lull before the storm. His father approached her almost tentatively then, ostensibly to commiserate over the death of dinner. He took the smouldering pot off the burner and gently steered her to the nearest chair. She sat down, but without the slightest softening of her face.

'That last resonating crash, Paro, was the wall coming down, once and for all. We could finally climb inside the space we could only see and wonder at earlier. I have told you it was half wild and half deliberately fashioned, like a hobbit's nest, or perhaps closer to a sanctuary for a tree sprite.' This took Deep aback; hadn't he thought his strange visitor tree-sprite-like the moment he saw her? 'But the most startling aspect,' his father continued, 'wasn't clear till we were actually in ...'

With his mother still in her stony state, Deep sought to end her misery. 'That resounding crash distracted her for just that moment I needed to gather my seven-year-old wits about me and run like only a frightened boy can. I scuttled down the stairs, scrambled across the landing to the next flight down, hearing all the while her footsteps behind me, but not the thundering kind I expected her new larger-than-life avatar to produce. They had gone back to being soft, almost musical with an alluring rhythm to them. But I didn't want to get sucked back in, so I dived headlong down those stairs!'

His mother let out a yelp. Jumping out of her chair, she flung herself across the room. 'How do I save this?' she cried, peering anxiously into her pot of ruined khichotto. Deep too had yelped when tumbling to a halt at a pair of feet. He had no doubt she could have flown to the bottom of the stairs before him, judging by all the inexplicable things she'd already done, but those were not her feet. Those large feet encased in sensible, now dusty, shoes belonged to his father. Who, having taken in the state of his son, shivering, scratched from his fall and festooned with cobwebs, scooped him up and carried him to where the workmen were still gaping at their discovery.

'From somewhere in the depths of the house, I heard the slam of a door and hoped fervently it was our visitor leaving. But for the most part, Baba and I were holding on to each other, transfixed by the sight before of us. Of this long-buried tree-born room. Then, still carrying me, Baba stepped in. The workmen followed, though more mystified and rattled than men of action like to admit to being. As we walked through it, skirting the odd pieces of rough-hewn furniture, musty sheets puddled in the middle and lanterns hanging at head-height, the clammy walls with their leafy decorations seemed to reach out and touch us as we passed. And then, very quickly (as it was only a tiny place really), we had traversed the scooped-out space and pushing past a cascade of twigs, emerged on the other side.'

'Into the sunshine,' supplied his father, 'underneath our mango tree.'

Deep stopped for breath to see his mother scraping the contents of the pot into the bin stoically, resigned to the loss of beliefs she had held dear for so long. Like being able to cook a good pot of khichotto. And knowing what goes on in her home. His father continued, 'We found ourselves on the exact spot I had seen Deep standing an hour earlier with the slip of a girl. The room we had walked through was half house and half mango tree in a way that I cannot, to this day, describe. Further digging with the aid of the workmen revealed that the mango tree had, over the years, welded itself to the side of our house, and the damp from the tree had seeped into a section of our walls, which is what we were repairing that day. Who was to know that between the tree and the house had grown a room?'

'And that someone lived in it,' said his mother accusingly. 'I knew nothing about that, Paro. All that week we were working on the invasion of moist ...' began his dad, but was stopped short by a glare from his mother.

Deep knew this was the beginning of a fight he did not want to see. They hadn't fought in years, to his knowledge, mostly because they sought refuge in concoctions and current events. Also known as cooking and newspapers, as it had been earlier that afternoon. So, while they were locked in their furious discussion about the room and god knows what else (Deep certainly didn't want to know), he wandered off outside to where the tree still stood, though now there was nothing where the room would have been. There were obvious repairs to the wall just behind it. A metal gate ran between wall and trunk, and Deep had never understood before why that might be. But before the door to his home shut behind him, he heard his mother ploughing into his dad for everything he had ever 'forgotten' to tell her in the thirty-five years they'd spent together.

Deep settled down under the tree, just where he remembered sitting with her that day. Or sort of remembered. A lot of the story he'd related that afternoon had come to him as he narrated it. His memory flooding back, but with a force and form engendered by the situation; his father's story of the room, his mother's obvious upset, and his own need to pin it down. It had, in the heat of the situation, been forged into something more real, yet more mysterious and frightening than he'd initially remembered. Not surprisingly, in the quiet of the garden at twilight, some of that had begun to recede and feel unreal. When he had decided to write about the incident for his university's Memory Project, all it had been was a flickering image of a conversation with an unknown young woman underneath their tree. Like the old black and white films it resembled, it was a disjointed memory. Sitting under the tree again, he went back to the starting point, which was the most vivid to him. Delicately pretty and unusually interested in them and their house, he had been sure she was the nanny from next door. Everything else would have to be re-examined for veracity in a less emotionally charged place.

So lost in thought was Deep, he hadn't realised his father had walked up to join him underneath the tree. He was twirling a glowing cigarette between his fingers like Deep knew he hadn't in fifteen years. But with the practised ease of a swimmer who hasn't forgotten how, he passed it to his son for a solitary drag. 'You know, I don't recall a room like that, don't you, Baba? Just a darkness beyond the demolished wall.'

'Yes, I know,' his father tilted his head forward in acceptance of the fact (and the image of Nearly Headless Nick flashed through Deep's mind again). Then, taking one last drag from his once-a-decade treat, he confessed, 'I don't either.'

NEVER ALONE

He jumped off the high branch, hollering. Falling, floating, dipping. Finally landing on top of the heap of arms and legs under the tree with enough force to make the owners of the limbs emit a collective groan. The boy who had scudded into them, rolled off the top, exhorting them to get up and get going as he straightened out his long and improbably ungainly limbs, was Billy. Billy the Brave, a natural-born leader, was ready to strike out again. There was no time to lose.

'The sun's shining, people, and we have lots left to do. Chop-chop!'

Sunny days were rare in the forest, and as much as could be made of it, should. The kids all understood this. Besides, Billy always knew best, and he always said it with a smile and a pat on the back for those who were doing their darnedest. Egging them on to shift their inert bodies off the ground, where they'd fallen from the branch above, just like him (but then chosen not to move, unlike him), he loped around them as he prodded. The mesh of arms and legs started to stir. And disentangle.

'But we're *so* tired, Billy,' pleaded Tiny Madeline, the littlest one.

Her translucent, sharp-boned face, spattered with mud from where she lay in a heap with the others at the bottom of the tree, hinted at their earlier exertions. Her cheeks were glowing and so was the tip of her nose. The high wind and brilliant sun in which they'd set out had whipped her extremities into a bright beacon red. The wind whistled through the forest constantly, but in the open, where they found themselves that morning after a few hours of threshing through undergrowth, it screamed like a banshee and pursued them. Across the open field and down swells, they stumbled in their haste to get away. And finally, up the tree with its wide, spreading branches, in which they took refuge. Temporarily. Till Billy insisted they move on. They dropped one by one to the ground, like apples past their prime. But they were children, not fruit-on-the-turn. They could still make something of the opportunity the day had brought.

Despite her protestations, Madeline was one of the first on her feet. The rest – the untidy bundle of twiggy limbs – untangled itself into various children more slowly. A rag-tag bunch, they were different sizes – adolescents alongside those barely out of toddlerhood. And different shades, though impossible to tell what, uniformly covered as they were in mud and grass. What they all had in common was their whippet leanness and nervous energy (except in the last few minutes when they'd barely moved from exhaustion). And that their clothes were torn to shreds – from the day's adventures, no doubt, any onlooker would have thought. They would have also supposed that the children would be in for a thorough reprimand when they got home. But the latter appeared to regard 'home', the house looming over them in the distance, with an anxiety beyond that of children afraid of a scolding.

'You see that high window?' Harry, one of the smallest but not youngest, and certainly amongst the wisest, said to Maddy. 'I feel something terrible rising inside me when I look at it.'

'Why?' Maddy asked, though she knew what he meant. This new home had brought with it a gamut of new experiences and emotions, not least now as they spent their days trying to reach the margin of the backwoods the house stood in. She knew instinctively why they were doing that. But it had never been said, not even by Billy, who was not usually afraid to speak out.

'Don't look now,' whispered Harry again, 'but that's why.'

Maddy couldn't help but look, and yet again, there was someone at the window. It didn't always seem to be the same person, but in the last weeks, a rumble had rolled through their pack, an unstated warning that someone new was manning the high window, and this one was stranger than any other. Lopsided, as if standing on one limb, this one had glowing discs for eyes, and a clicking call that frightened them. The children had more reason than ever to keep their eyes fixed on the prize of the finish line.

(2)

The lopsided, disc-eyed monster at the window wasn't thinking of grisly things to do to the children at all. He, Herman, was thinking how much he'd like to join them. Join them in running free through the sunlit countryside. They looked a bit winded at the end of each day of frenetic activity, but anything would be better than being stuck in that cheerless room. He, Herman, Herman Alone, was in the room at the top of the house that had a single dirt-splashed window, overlooking the fields and forests. A window that allowed its watcher to see farther, over the tops of the moss-green trees, than anyone else in the quiet, nearly concealed house. In turn, it was the only window that could be spied from the ground, with every other shrouded by dense foliage. Anyone looking out could see the children. But the children couldn't look into the darkness past the dull glint of panes. Into the lower storeys, they couldn't see at all. Which did not mean there was nothing there; they did, after all, have a dim recollection of people who had looked after them before their release. Those half-remembered people faded further from the minds of the youthful horde with every passing day – so quietly kind, yet unremarkable, had they been. But the window at the top gleamed in the sun like a flare, attracting attention. And as new faces appeared at it, each watching them closer than was comfortable, it had the effect the unknown has on all humans. It engendered fear. As if by design.

And if *they* were acutely aware of watchers at the window, the latter too, by a trick of placing, found the presence of the children more overwhelming than was physically true. More immediate certainly than the people who lived on the floors below. Though, especially in the evenings, an almost constant murmur from below stairs would reach their ears. The strange new boy listened as if his life depended on it.

'We did our best by them.'

'And now, we have to get our broken-winged boy ready to fly.'

'Shall we have chicken for dinner tonight?'

Still, they were blurs compared to the running, jumping, vital children he watched all day, till sundown wrapped shadows around them. Herman decided it was time to try to make contact with them again. Painfully shifting his plaster-cast leg so he could shuffle up to the window, he ended up upturning the dregs of the swill brought up to him earlier. And was immediately worried that the clatter had been heard downstairs. Would it bring Lily flying up to his room, her face scrunched up with anxiety? When he'd accidentally dropped his spoon with a reverberating clang, two nights before, Lily had come huffing and puffing up the stairs, chuntering unhappily to herself, 'Why do they do this to me – why?? Don't I feed and shelter them? Don't

I take them away from their miserable lives? Is there no gratitude left in the world?' Then, lifting her perpetually narrowed eyes from its scrutiny of the floorboards, she harangued him, but gently, 'Do you not see everything we do for you? That of all our children, we have coddled you the most?' Afraid to blurt out the wrong answer, Herman gaped in disc-eyed horror, till with a disappointed twist of her thin lips, she clumped back down again. 'No words,' she muttered, as she descended. 'Drive me into the ground with worry, why don't you?'

Herman, Herman Alone, took a deep breath and wondered what about him worried her so much – he could barely move. He wasn't about to go anywhere. Except closer to the window. He grabbed the arms of the only other chair in the room and heaved himself to it, placing his face against the cool pane to take his mind off the other insistent ache – the agony of his broken leg. The kids below had never responded to the steady tap-tap of his fingers on the window before. So, this time, he laid his palm against the window, pulling it back in that familiar about-to-slap action which had marked every evening of his young life till his move to this house. Then, he gave it a hard thwack. But not so hard he would damage the already-brittle glass, and bring more reproach in its wake.

This time, someone *did* hear. Madeline, or Pale Face as he thought of her, looked around and realised it had come from the high window, her eyes widening in wonder when she finally spotted him. With her little mouth open in a surprised 'o', she tugged urgently at the sleeve of the older boy beside her. They both looked up then. All this, Herman could clearly see. Him. Herman. Herman Alone. For a fleeting moment, Alone No Longer. That was the other thing that gnawed at him – how lucky they were to be together, and why couldn't he be? 'Well, you know,' Lily's partner, Alan, had said to him ponderously, 'that's why you were sent here, because you couldn't rub along.'

'It was just the once,' he'd answered back, and received a weary sigh in response; Lily's.

'It won't happen again, I promise.'

'That is why you are where you are, taking time to heal, to learn not to make that mistake again,' Alan assured, and Lily cooed to end the conversation, 'You'll be running with those children soon enough, my boy!'

That was weeks ago. But now, at the near-acknowledgement of his presence by the children below, he got excited enough to attempt to stand up to wave to them. Nothing had roused him quite so much in a long time – friends, he might have made friends! But in doing so, he landed with a crash, half in, half out of the chair he was in. Yet, the pain he felt from jarring his broken leg didn't bother Herman half as much as the look he'd seen on the kids' faces as he came crashing down. He knew that look. He'd caught it in passing – in mirrors, car windows, and metallic utensils – often enough. With that expression on their faces, they could have been extensions of himself, but that was not the kind of kinship he wanted. Nor could he understand why they looked with such fear at his face at the window. It unsettled him. Worse, their fearful looks soon turned to panic as they turned and ran. Why, oh why, he thought, subsiding into being Just Herman again. Herman Alone.

He wasn't left wondering about their inexplicable reaction for long, as Alan entered the room, sombre and steady, the opposite of fluttering, prattling Lily. With three large steps, he was atop Herman. The latter, expecting a meaty fist to slam into him next, as on every other night at his many 'homes', wrapped his own stick-thin arms around himself in anticipation. But he only got picked up in Big Alan's arms, who, with a gentle admonishing shake, placed him carefully, almost decorously, back into his chair by the window. 'Stay there, this time,' the big man rumbled (grumbled even, but indulgently), as he walked away. 'Your time to shine will come.'

The stairs creaked in protest as he made his way down, which left Herman Alone wondering if it could have been his own puny frame that had frightened the children so, or something more substantial.

(3)

The children scrambled over the scrub, towards the next hurdle they'd promised themselves they would cross that day – the deep, dark brook at the bottom of the overgrown prickly meadow they had spent half the morning traversing. Their aim, as outlined by Billy as they'd sat around their dwindling fire the previous night, was to get as close to the line that marked the end of their world, as they could. So, they kept their eyes peeled on the blue-green horizon as they ran, but the line shifted, blurred, mocked them, and never seemed to get any closer. When night fell, their time would be up – they knew that from experience – and they would have to retreat to safe places. Spend the nocturnal hours when hope had been extinguished with the sun, in a hideout usually set up by the older children, always checked by the stalwart Bobby for its safety, till the sun peeped out and a day where all things were possible, even getting to the end of the line, had begun. That perhaps it wasn't actually possible, because they had never managed it, didn't strike them. They were children after all, even never-say-die Billy, and hope never perished in their hearts. But the sun was still shining, and today of all days, it may have been possible to cross the stream and see what lay beyond. See the real world again, reach out, touch and rejoin it.

'And one day, the end will come,' they remembered the lady saying to them affectionately, 'and you will be released from your troubles.'

'Even see your folks again,' the usually morose man had winked and smiled.

They didn't know what that meant, as they'd never had any. But that promise meant everything to them; it was what they hung on to every day, and worked towards. Like at that moment.

Billy, oldest, fastest, most resilient of them all, was running at the head of the pack. He was the only one who remained unfazed by the obstacles that had come their way – the strange ivy that wound its way around their young limbs when they weren't watching, the little puddles that turned out fathoms deep if you accidentally got a foot in, or the sunlight which tricked you into sleep if you let it seep in for too long, and thus, lose hours and hours in the day. Ever alert to these dangers, Billy was still shouting them on, encouraging the littlest ones trailing behind, with every puff of hard-won breath in the steadily dampening air. Then, out of the greying blue, the hair at the nape of his neck stood up like hackles. A warning that some of his cohorts were down. Exhausted. Not able to go on. Especially the little ones, with their blister-pocked feet and rumbling tummies. Over the many weeks he'd been their helmsman, he could sense when they flagged even if he couldn't see, and steered them to safer waters when it got choppy. Now, he flung exhortations behind him, letting the whippy wind carry them:

'C'mon Timmy, my man, pick yourself up, fella.'

'Maddy, my Madeline, keep running, keep running. You're the best.'

And the last one, that was only half heard as Billy tried to take a flying leap over the narrow but furiously bubbling stream, plunging to the bottom instead – 'Harry, no one does it better than you, speed up as you come up to the bank of the stream and …'

Bubble, bubble, glub, glub. Arms flailing. Wet straw-coloured hair spread like seaweed on the surface. Long limbs thrashing through water. And then submerged. Every last bit. Digits. Tendrils. Shirt tails. Till nothing at all of him could be seen. For a few seconds that felt like hours, everyone stood still. And silent. Then Madeline screamed, 'Help him! Save him!' The older boys fanned out around the stream tentatively. They knew they should help. If there was anyone they would have helped, it was Billy, who had seen them that far, but they were petrified of jumping into that opaque water. Scared limb-locked by what was sucking Billy in as they watched.

'What's in there?' Charlie asked, afraid.

'Billy, it's Billy. Help him!' Little Madeline cried out again.

'No,' said Charlie, barely audible in his fright, 'there's something 'neath him.'

'Holding on to his feet,' whispered another child, hanging back and haunted.

'It's this THING,' Charlie said, conclusively. His chubby face closed to possibilities, now that Billy wasn't around to prise it open.

But who would prise open the grip that held Billy under water? He had been struggling valiantly against whatever it was. Now, he stopped. Under the crusty layer of scum on the surface, nothing could be seen, so Harry crept up close, screwing up his courage to do so. Little Harry, much younger than many of the older children frozen in fear, tentatively broke the crust on the water. Then, he dipped his fingers in, followed by his toes. As he did, something splashed in its depths and the other children jumped back. Looking around him to see if anyone would join him in his attempt to save their leader, he realised there would be no help from anywhere but Little Madeline, who was already rolling up her dungaree legs. Together, they looked closely into the water. Their noses almost touching the scum atop. They could see murk. They saw darkness, and shifting shadows that could be currents. But currents that strong in a piddling backwoods stream? And definitely no Billy. That was reason enough to wade in, though the pack murmured warnings from as far up the bank as they could go.

'Don't go, don't go on,' hissed Charlie, but Madeline was having none of it. If it wasn't for Billy, she would have gone under long ago, but if she did it now, it would be for the best cause in the world, she decided. As she held her nose and immersed herself, Harry breathed, 'Wait for me, I'm coming in,' disappearing beneath the murk too. On the embankment, the children watched silently. There were all kinds of quiet amongst them. Fear was its most prevalent cause, but there was also exasperation that they weren't just leaving Billy to his fate and running for the horizon as was the plan. They scanned the water for the heroic duo who had followed their chief in. Yet, Maddy and Harry must have bored down so deep, there wasn't a ripple or a break in the water to be seen.

Then, there was. Just the smallest ebb. A tiny rip in its watery fabric. A smudge of a shadow that grew and grew. But of the three humans in the water, not a sign. When the onlookers had almost given up, a body floated up, as if released by the spirits of the depths. It was Billy, and following not far behind, keeping him moored, were the two tykes. They were all blanched out by the water, dripping, otherworldly. But Billy looked bloated and grotesque besides, like something had crawled under his skin. He was also completely still, not thrashing, not swimming, and not drowning any more. The youthful mob on the bank went from petrified and silent to seething and discontented the minute Maddy and Harry's stick-thin arms managed to haul him to the shore. Billy was back. But Billy could no longer lead. Billy was useless then, wasn't he? They needed a new leader who would get them where they needed to go. To that green-blue line that was ever-shifting. But would it shift no longer, now that Billy was gone? Would it be the beginning of a new dawn, and a new brace of possibilities?

As with any mob, all their troubles were suddenly pinned on their dead leader. He had become so dispensable, most of them turned their backs on him. The line was shifting. It would be impenetrable and shrouded from the eye by night-time, and they had no time to lose.

(4)

The boy at the window watched this drama unfold. That he could see over the tops of the trees, all the way to the horizon, delighted him at first, but then, Herman began to worry that he, Herman, him and him alone, had been placed there for a purpose. He wasn't sure by whom, really. Maybe God. His foster parents, all forty of them, would have said so. He wondered if it meant he would be called upon to do something. Something heroic nobody thought him capable of, least of all, him. Or a more sacrificial role perhaps, he considered, and was overcome with terror that this seemed more suitable for him.

For most of the life he could remember, he had been bounced from family to family, from home to home. His clumsiness had always been held against him, or he was too solitary, too silent, too ugly, too thin, or just about anything that could be held against a child. So, they would let him go, to make his way to the next home, and then the next, till at the last one, it hadn't been any of the old complaints against him, but that he was 'a threat'. He didn't understand what he'd done to intimidate, four-foot-three and twig-limbed as he was, but that had been the last nail in his coffin, so to speak, and he had arrived at this final destination. 'We will never let you go,' his new foster mother had said to him, affectionately enough, but so unused was he to it, it had kept him up for weeks. And on those nights, in a room so bare, talk from below permeated through the boards, he heard Alan and Lily discuss him in terms that should have gladdened any neglected kid's heart.

'Isn't he perfect?' Lily almost gurgled with glee.

'The boy we always wanted,' Alan growled. 'He won't be the trouble some of the others have been.'

'And when the time comes, he will head out without much fuss I feel,' Alan concluded, basing his hunch on his years of experience of taking in strays and waifs.

'Ah, yes,' sighed Lily, 'and I will, as always, find it hard to lose them, even as I delight in their freedom from their earthly sorrows.'

Herman heard Alan agree, 'We do for them what no one else will.'

Conditioned to be suspicious, however, from years of mistreatment in foster homes, their wan ward didn't give in to the relief and prickling fondness that pushed at his heart. They confused him with their concern and calculating watchfulness, all at once. He had understood before he was moved there that the home he was being sent to specialised in physically and emotionally 'damaged' children. More and more of these kids had been sent to them, as each settled down, and became a part of the landscape. Never again sticking out like the sore thumbs all fostered children seemed to be. Social services loved this home for their difficult ones because they never had to worry about them again, as Lily did all the keeping in touch, reporting back without exception, with glowing progress reports. How they had almost 'got to the finish line'. How quite a few triumphed, becoming 'one with the world'. And for the occasional child who didn't, she had infinite patience. They, too, would make her proud one day. In the meantime, they kept their stomachs full and teeth clean.

Listening to these transformation tales and doubting he could ever be one, Herman had been glad to see the triumphant troupe, nevertheless. Outside, where they'd obviously been allowed to wander as a reward for their 'rubbing along'. That thing he was finding hard to do. And so, he rattled around, alone, in the echoing house. Him alone, Alone Herman. Or he would rattle if he could move. But locks, steps and casts ensured he couldn't. He couldn't be sure he was the only child left in, but he sensed it from the house's graveyard silence. Beyond his window though, and pouring through its thin glass, were giggles, cries and bellowed encouragement, so insistent that it had pushed him to look out the window properly for the first time and feel connected. From then on, he had painfully dragged himself to it every morning to be closer to them. He could smile at them all morning; he so loved watching them run free. His heart leapt, skipped and tumbled with them on their enviable daily adventures.

Yet, he had also begun to notice how their devil-may-care demeanour was not altogether pleasant. Their wild hair and long nails, with teeth glinting sharply from so far away, put an otherworldly pall on their appearance. But living free might do that, he argued with himself. He had to admit, too, that the terrain that looked so gorgeously green and sun-drenched in the mornings, never looked as hospitable at night. Not for the likes of him, he surmised. The length of the view from his window and how closely he felt the children's presence as a result, soon began to worry rather than delight him, and his desperate desire to join them began to fade. Wasn't this vastness offered up to him, strange? When in every other way, his world had shrunk?

(5)

As the children drifted off, with Billy's body still lying sodden on the ground, Madeline called out, 'Wait. We should bury him.'

'Christian rituals,' Jared, the oldest boy left, sneered, 'in this place?'

'What would you suggest then, Jay?' asked Harry, in all seriousness.

'Push him back into the water?' chirped a girl. 'That's what Vikings do, you know.'

'Not Vikings,' jeered another rowdy boy, 'just mermaids.'

'No, not the water,' Charlie pointed, whispering. They could all see then that whatever had sucked Billy in, was still waiting. There were tiny bubbles floating to the top and a shadow beneath, palpitating though barely discernible. The rowdy boy, playing at pushing other kids in, gave Charlie the first shove, then tugged at a little girl. It wasn't long before the other children had joined the angry, confused scrum, and chaos engulfed the embankment.

'Stop, stop!' entreated Maddy in distress, as Billy, lying misshapen and motionless, was forgotten. As her piercing little voice sliced through the fog of resentment, carrying all the way to the boy in the window, he leaned forward to get a better view. Watching for weeks, he had only just begun to see clearly.

'Well,' little Harry said when the dust had settled, 'if not in the land or under water, then where?'

From behind all the other children, rose a plaintive plea, 'We could eat him.'

It came from the child always hanging back, muttering to himself. Thin and feral, it struck the others that they had never seen him joining in their foraged meals. What *had* he been eating all that time? They were only one child down before Billy, and little Letitia, who died of a fever, had been buried ... hadn't she? The children shifted nervously, giggled, and made to shuffle along. The hungry kid, with his terribly timed joke, did not worry them as much as the increased scrutiny of the watcher at the window. He had undoubtedly swooped closer to it, like a vulture homing in on prey. Why did he watch them so carefully, they'd asked each other before, but now they wondered if he didn't just watch, but controlled them too?

When the first drops of rain fell, while they were still arguing Billy's fate, they looked up at the lowering sky, and at the suddenly lit lamp at the high window, searching for answers the blank face of the house did not yield. Living in it seemed like so long ago, they could barely remember their past lives. As the rain came down in knife-edged sheets, they finally ran for cover, trusting that one of them would deal with the body (now, just the body, Billy no more). But when all had left the open ground around the murky pond, a pair of thin shoulders slouched back. The weaselly boy, having made the decision no one else could, dragged Billy's body away, disappearing with it into the undergrowth.

(6)

No one noticed but Herman. Herman Alone. Shocked, he recoiled from the window, only to fall with a resounding crash that brought footsteps to his door.

'You poor dear,' Lily cried, and rushing to him, pulled him up by his twiggy arms. 'What happened, my little one?' she asked, her eyes brimming with tears. Her vast body trembled too, as if with suppressed sobs, so moved was she by his plight. Behind her, he heard clearly, the lumbering tread of Alan coming up the stairs. Already shaken, Herman wanted nothing more than to be rid of them both. Exemplary-care record aside, no other foster couple had ever had such honeyed words for him or evinced such concern, and yet, their clucking presence did nothing to comfort him. He wished fervently he could lock the door on them. Or better still, lock them into the bare room with the high window, and fly like the wind out of those grounds. And suddenly, he saw in her face that she knew this too. That she had always known he'd never completely bought it.

She stepped back, her face transformed. The mask had come swiftly off, but Alan still stood behind her with his face composed to gently scold and commiserate. Lily turned to him – 'You know what? I think he's ready.'

'Do you think, my dear?' Alan probed, his face still seamed with concern. 'There isn't much for a boy who can't run. Slim pickings out there, some days.'

'He is ready,' she asserted, breathing heavily, with an excitement she no longer bothered to hide. 'He won't be able to run like the others, run with the sun, run like the wind. He will traverse a different path, instead, but oh, it will be beautiful.'

As she got more and more poetic about his fate, a change came over Alan, too. For the first time since Herman had met him, he began to laugh. It was a loud, boisterous belly laugh. It shook the single windowpane. It nearly shook the room. 'Oh, oh, oh,' he guffawed, 'what fun it'll be!'

What had seemed to be Lily's suppressed sobs, turned out to be stifled laughter, as she joined Alan openly – 'Imagine. He'll be dragging himself along, trying to get away. But oh no, no chance. He'll barely last a day!'

'If the land don't get ya,' Alan said, directly to Herman then, cackling into his face, 'one of our half-starved babes will. Broken bones won't bother them.'

'And for once,' bayed Lily, like a hyena, her face incandescent with joy, 'it won't matter that he'll never get through our mazes, never get far enough to fall into our traps, or try unendingly to reach the end of a course we know can't be nixed. It will be a brilliant new adventure – for all of us!'

'Because what we love to see, above all else,' Alan said, quietening down, his face folding back into the picture of anxious concern it had been five minutes before, 'is children released from the troubles of this world.'

'Yes,' agreed Lily, softly, sobering up in a trice, like the uproarious laughter of the preceding moments had never happened, 'and you, my dear Herman, will get there sooner than any other child we've had here. Becoming one with the elements in no time.'

Watching, terrified, as the once-again gently concerned couple saw themselves out of the bare room with its high window, Herman, Herman Alone, of all the children who'd been through that door, knew what lay in wait for him on the morrow. But as he thought over the life he'd had, his fear dissipated, and he smiled. He would never be alone again.

LOVE RATS

R ani thought a breath of fresh air would do her good.
This particular assignation wasn't going to plan. The
room felt too brightly lit, the pictures on the wall too
impersonally cubic, the traffic crawling like ants way down
below. All of it faceless. As ineffectual as the man fidgeting
impatiently beside her, as she stood at the window, looking
down, because there just didn't seem to be anything to say.
She'd tried a few times and drawn a blank.

'The colours in a room, they can make a difference,
can't they?' she thought out loud, looking at the icy blue of
the walls that was freezing her to the marrow. Or it might
have been his conversation.

'Oh, uhuh, do they?'

So undeniably disinterested, it shut off another avenue
of chatter that could have led to something less superficial.
But then, he touched her sleeve and she turned to him,

expecting a flash of humour, or wry everyday wisdom. 'Let's get our kits off,' he said, instead.

Aaaand that pretty much kills it, mister, she thought. How to say that though? How, when you've been brought up to be polite even to the person who steps on your toes in their rush to beat you to the front of the line, as happened just that morning on the tram there? 'Sorry,' she'd mumbled then, as if it had been her fault. 'Sorry,' she almost said now, but bit her tongue in time.

'How about a cup of tea?' she offered. Adding brightly, 'And then maybe you can tell me more about yourself.'

She knew immediately she sounded like his maiden aunt, but that wasn't a bad thing. She wasn't quite feeling him, after all. Though feel him, hold him, taste him, was what she was expected to do in such situations. These new situations she'd signed up to a couple of months ago, because she was tired of waiting for her husband to come home. Waiting for him to spend the evening, laughing with her, pulling her into his arms, nuzzling her neck, as he delivered extravagant compliments about her eyes, hair, smell even. None of which had happened in a good, long while. 'You okay?' he might ask, as he'd look in on an evening, on his way to some other meeting, conference, powwow. Or assignation?

A question she had begun to ask herself so often, that in the end, in a fit of pique and an ocean of despair, she'd signed up for just that. A service for married folks that helped them find other people with whom they could recreate those early, heady days of being a couple. Or that's what she thought she was subscribing to when she first came across it, while desultorily surfing the net for clubs to join. Warm, genial, and of course, tasteful, is how it appeared. And the service's app, gemlike and glowing on her phone, promised *so* much.

'Won't find my way in, will I, with all those layers in the way?' said the strangely eager yet distant man in the room, reminding her of all that this gig was not. Wincing a little, she heard the disgusted voice of her Shoulder Devil bark, 'Why don't you just leave him?'

'Just about to,' she replied, thinking her SD meant the man she'd found herself unhappily contemplating canoodling with. Then she understood it was her husband the sprite meant. But that was the whole point of doing this, she argued, wasn't it? This time, she turned to Shoulder Angel for support, but the latter was snoozing. As had increasingly been the case since Rani signed up. 'Oi!' she prodded it, but when the man in the room stopped his precipitate stripping, she wondered if she'd said it aloud. No, she wasn't cheating on her husband because she wanted to leave, but because she didn't! Which part of that was hard to understand, she rolled her eyes at her sprites. Rani hoped the answer to her marriage conundrum lay in biding her time with other men while she tried to understand what had gone wrong with the one she loved (and might not things learnt from other men help her do that?). It would also take the edge off her disappointment with him, allowing her to step away from her suspicions about his smoke and mirror pursuits which were eating her alive (and wasn't it, therefore, revenge, too, for his many absences and more slights?). It would furnish her as well with the warmth that was missing from her life. She wrote all this down, and then playing Portia against herself, argued and counter-argued every rationale, till she had persuaded herself of the wisdom of her actions. Finally, registering herself for this frightening, intriguing 'service' on a sunless and decidedly confused afternoon.

What she really wanted was to be admired. Understood. Loved. And so, a series of trysts in pretty boutique hotels followed, where all she had to do was allow them to paw her a little, while she sipped a long, tall drink, and wondered where to get the gorgeous wrought-iron headboards that graced every room (and wasn't it useful no bonking happened, 'coz unyielding iron and violently thrown-back heads don't mix, she told SA after). But this one, this cut-to-the-chase fella, he just didn't get it.

'How about it now?' He broke into her reverie, and she noted with both shock and interest that he'd shed all in the time it had taken her to remind herself why she was there. Their relative states of dishabille made a change though, from every film, ad and event plastered with naked women, abundantly oozing out, while the men sat around as distantly buttoned observers. She was the observer in this instance, but it was amazement rather than lust that had got her goggle-eyed. In every other 'situation' she had found herself in, it hadn't got to this (phew, exhaled SA). On a really good day, the early, easy chatter could forge a powerful enough connect for her to want to see the man again. And maybe even allow that little bit of fondling. This was not the point of her meetings though, she told SD sternly, but the bonus. Bonus. Boners. Points. Plus points. They could be that, but not this time. And she would have to make her position, or lack of interest in getting into one, clear.

'Back in a jiffy with that tea!' she trilled, collecting the little that *she*'d shed, namely bag and jacket, on her way to the door. 'If you are that desperate for tea, lady ...' she heard him grumble in response, as she shut the door on his quickly wilting bits. Walking away from her shiny, bland room and equally vanilla hook-up, Rani amused herself thinking of all the ways, either offensive or inane, in which that sentence might have ended, deciding magnanimously that what he was really going to say next was that he had a packet of relaxing green tea, which he'd whip out for her (instead of the thing he did) and set brewing. She looked over her shoulder to check he hadn't followed, because the last thing she wanted was to be spotted in broad daylight leading strange naked men, like the Pied Piper of Love Rats, down the characterless corridors of that huge, industrial hotel. Big, bright and self-absorbedly busy as it was, it was bound to have prying eyes. With mirrors to show you up and revolving doors to usher you out. Endlessly anonymous rooms and passages, and uniformity wherever you looked. Like dating with apps.

The bizarre thing was that everyone she'd met off the website, agreed. Yet, there they all were. All craving the kind of connection these sites didn't cater for. 'I'm part of the furniture now,' one balding man had cried on her shoulder. And that was all the squelch of that particular rendezvous, but at least she understood where it was coming from. Her prospective bedfella though, not so much. Was he even married? Didn't everyone on that app have to be? But he had a six-pack. Like, not six rolls of fat, but firm muscle. Reason enough for suspicion, as no married person ever had a taut tummy, and didn't she know it! No, he wasn't right somehow, especially that bit where he looked into her large, limpid eyes but failed to compliment her on them. Those little spots of buttering up literally greased her joints and made all things possible. 'Those eyes make me melt,' the last one had said to her. 'Your smile is pure sunshine,' and even the less poetic 'What a lovely figure you *still* have,' did the job too, on occasion. With this latest one, however, there was neither gooey admiration nor warm cerebral effusions to hold them together. But they *had* chosen each other, she marvelled, as she marched down another corridor, by both swiping lazily with a forefinger in the same direction. What a strange premise on which to base the most intimate of activities, she sighed, as she stumbled into an unnerving oasis of mirrors from which corridors radiated in every direction. Corridors without apparent ends. Like these purposeless encounters she found herself in. And a morning maybe wasted. But she still had to decide which passageway to go down, even just to finish with it.

The mirrors, however, turned out to be lift doors. Not pointless after all. She took a minute to stare at the many incarnations of Rani being reflected back at her to decide what to do. She could push the button that would take her to the hotel's large, shiny foyer, and back out into the bustle of the world, without telling Buff Boy that she was off. Or she could go back to their room. But you don't need to, hissed SD, because you very sensibly remembered to grab your new jacket before you left the room. Rani realised she also had her handbag, for those cups of tea she meant to buy, of course. She really could disappear into the ether, but something held her back. Was it that she didn't know how it would go down in the brave new world she'd signed up to? If she were to stop altogether, would she miss the handholding and sympathy? Perhaps with her particular needs, it struck her, she would be better placed in a book club than a website for sexual skulduggery. At any rate, her innate niceness told her to go back and tell him she couldn't go through with it. She couldn't ghost him after all (but a little crumbing never hurt anyone, breathed SD).

The lift doors opened to reveal the hotel concourse widening into a flashy mall-like ground floor, where half the city milled and mooched. You were less noticeable when everybody was there already, Rani estimated, as she stepped out, and not a single soul up to any good. Precisely why it was the right choice for illicit assignations, more often than the shady hotels of films, or the intimate little ones of her liking. It may not have worked for her but in the buzz surrounding her, she sensed satisfaction and industry. Lost in her thoughts, she realised too late she was about to plough into some hapless fellow.

'Rani,' he stammered from the shock of seeing her at this hotel, of all places. His brain foggy from the night's exertions, he hadn't clocked the familiar head bobbing towards him. Especially as the streaks in them were completely new and he'd barely been home long enough to notice. Busy as he'd been, checking himself in the procession of mirrors for visible signs of having been at it all week, he didn't see her till they'd actually collided. The blanching of both their faces as a result could have put the anaemic hotel walls to shame.

'Arnie?' she spluttered in return.

Arnab, or Arnie to friends, had strolled into the foyer at exactly the same moment as his wife. He had stepped out of the room he'd been in since last night (though he'd have said otherwise if pressed) for a breather too. With the drapes drawn in his room, the windows steamed up after their long night, and everything flung around, or settling in fusty heaps, he needed fresh air and perspective before he could plunge back in again. Even as he looked at his wife's face, momentarily focused on what looked like guilt and remorse, in his mind's eye swam the detritus of the activity in his room. Empty bottles, cigarette butts, smoke still hanging heavy in the stale air. And stains everywhere. Smudges from rifling fingers and imprints of lips clamped in concentration. All of which had begun to feel stifling in the morning. Not that he meant to abandon any of it. Oh no. He was enjoying himself, as he always did in these situations, he had said to a mirror in passing, smoothing down his mussed-up hair. Gone that way from the multiple times digits had been dragged through the strands, leaving them standing. His cheeks were recovering their colour too, from the prospect of the exciting hours ahead. But why on earth did his wife, his placid wife, look all shook up? He scrutinised her as best as he could from behind bleary eyes.

'You, you, you,' he blathered, 'you are here?'

'Um, erm, yes,' confessed a shamefaced Rani, and rummaging in her mind for a plausible reason, she announced, 'I'm here with my new book club.'

He felt the first stirrings of curiosity about her in a long while. But as she embarked on a convoluted explanation about the book club she had joined, he felt a creeping resentment too. This was his hideout. The place he went to when he needed to get away, stowing like a squirrel in its anonymous rooms whatever was most important to him at the time. In the last week, he'd been there a lot with his latest obsession. One that he didn't want his everyday world intruding into. And not his wife, most of all! Why was she really here? Didn't she look as furtive as he had in the mirror, moments ago? She couldn't be here for … no, no, she couldn't, he told himself firmly. Although there was that hair, and the whiff of a strange scent. But had she just evolved after he'd stopped noticing? And the book club? What extremes of boredom must have driven her to that! It was his fault and slowly, slowly, he must extricate himself from this other life, so he could pay her the attention she deserved.

But not now. Not yet. It was time to return. Immensely important things awaited. Rani would just have to understand. Again. 'Er, must go.'

'Book club too, eh?' she whispered ruefully, as he tried to make out what she meant, if she meant anything at all. An abrupt 'Well, bye then,' and they had crossed each other awkwardly, and were on their way. Yet, something about this inconsequential meeting in a hotel corridor felt momentous. Like the end was nigh. Or a new beginning was in the offing. It meant that he was more consumed with the need to finish what he'd started than ever. Because finish he must. That it came to him in Prannoy Roy's voice, as it always did in a crisis, did not strike him as nearly as strange as the imaginary creatures forever perched on his wife's shoulders. Now how weird is that, he said to himself. Rushing off, however, he saw something in her face that was weirder still. A sidelong glance quickly averted that made him question everything he thought he knew, and everything he was about to do.

Back in his room, he was overcome once more with elation over the developments that had engulfed his life these last few weeks. Tiptoeing to the bed, he looked down at the sprawl. Limbs and sheets. Creases and stains. The unmistakeable reek of wrongdoing filled the room, and he had to admit, it turned him on. If it filled him with trepidation too, he wasn't quite sure why. He shook his partner awake.

'Whaaaat?' she asked drowsily. Not ready for more, clearly, but he was.

'C'mon, we don't have all day. If we miss this window, who knows how many months, yes months, it might be before we get another chance.'

She smiled up at him lazily then, amused by how seriously he was taking it all. To her, it was just another of his mad chases for that intangible something that always eluded him. Arnie and his capers were amusing, but she could sense he thought this was make or break. 'Oh, okay then, let's get on with it.' She sat up, yawning, and sheets and sheets went flying to different corners of the room. Arnie chased after them, restoring them to the stack on the bed. They would be lost to the world over the next few hours, as they worked these sheets together. But not like this, not quite like this.

He put his arms around her then. Tightly. Lifting her clear off the bed, because what he wanted more than anything was nestling underneath her. On the reams and reams of paper she had been lying on was information so sensitive it could change the world in a day. Sheets and sheets of cheats they had begun to call that cascading stack. His partner-in-crime, as he thought of her, partner-in-uncovering-crime, at any rate, often joined him in this bland, bustling hotel to help with hush-hush assignments like this one. But this one was special. This was not one of his hyperlocal microscopic stings relating to the misdelivery of packages, or vets gone jab-mad. After a decade of local scoops, he'd finally landed the big one. It will shake the world, he told himself dramatically, and only he had the dope on it! But not for long, so he would have to hurry. Networks around the world were waiting for him to spill the beans. Waiting on him. For his world-changing beans. He felt powerful. It felt orgasmic. But for that tiny seed of worry which had grown – doubled – since he'd bumped into Rani. Yet, this was not the time to give in to doubt. Once more unto the breach, my son, Arnie heard Prannoy urge. Time to topple governments. Change lives. And he might just get to shake his own up too.

Sometime in the night, as the information began trickling in from the other side of the planet, from a hacker shacked up in Uzbekistan, his team started scrolling through it. She was now rolling out the long sheets of paper like toilet roll. Peering hard at the millions of tiny names spat out from the printer. Names from a whole network of websites that had been held in confidence all this time. Websites whose activities touched upon the rawest of human nerves, not illegal and yet illicit, dealing in betrayals. Streaming across the blue and into their hands were the names of every customer these sites had ever held, and then some, loosely linked to them. And on this humongous roll of dishonour were some very important people indeed, from what they could see. A very big coup for a very small news team! But Arnie hadn't looked at the names yet. Their wordsmith and their frontman, he was furiously stringing the sentences together that would deliver what he hoped would be a sucker punch to the system. Let his partner trawl through the thousands first, sending the important ones his way, and he would read them after. With thousands of names in this repository of lapsed spouses, as anyone who'd even harboured the notion had been snagged, he planned to rattle half the world, but only expose the handful who, in their hypocritical appropriation of the moral high ground, had for decades held political and religious sway. He knew that the tack they took on it – serious or salacious, censorious or forgiving – would colour audience perception ever after. Serious, said Prannoy to him sternly, and in this case, censorious. Give those sanctimonious politicians hell. Having just finished his script with a flourish, Arnie nodded happily. He was ready.

Yet, somewhere out there, his teammate Bobby was still grinding away at a sting. In flushing out one of the website's customers, he hoped to add human interest to their story. Remember, it's an important report and there has to be sacrificial lambs, Bobby had blustered, and Arnie had acquiesced. With so much else on his mind, curbing Bobby was not a priority. So he had left the young man to choose his own victim from the tide of customer names coming in, confident that nothing would come of it. Because with Bobby, nothing ever did.

Rani was thinking of sacrifice too as she walked slowly back to her room. That perhaps she had sacrificed enough for Arnie already, and maybe it was time to throw the marriage into the sacrificial pit too. 'But no,' urged SA, 'no, no that's not what you want and you know it.' 'He lies all the time though,' reminded SD. 'He's here, see? He's

here to cheat, because isn't this place Infidelity Central?'
But is he really, wondered Rani. That question had dogged
her down the passages and up the lift after their encounter.
He had said he was working, and he did look exhausted.
'Well, y'know,' smirked SD, 'rambunctious sex can do
that.' Oh yes, Rani sighed, trying to bat the unsettling
vision away, which small-time journalist exposing local
corruption needed to hole up in a hotel after all? Yet, if
he had been working all this time instead of canoodling,
she would never forgive herself. She might feel it in her
bones that he was cheating, but her heart wished fervently
it wasn't so. Amongst other things, she had the weight
of her own misdemeanours to carry now and she didn't
know if she could, alone. Even to the end of the too-bright
corridor. But there she was. Standing outside the door, and
counting to three. Would Buff Boy mind she hadn't come
back with tea? Since that wasn't what he'd been gagging
for, obviously. Then it struck her he may not even be there
still. Rani turned the handle and walked in to find him
naked and yakking into his phone with more animation
than she thought him capable.

'You're back,' he almost beamed as he hung up, and she
felt an additional pang of guilt. 'Um yes,' she admitted, 'I
got waylaid by a man on my way to the café.'

'Oh yeah?' he asked, suddenly interested. 'But that's
what you do, don't you?' Wrongfooted by his unexpectedly
intrusive question, she attempted to defend herself, 'No,
actually, not a lot. I'm fairly new to it.'

'And the man I saw in the corridor was my husband.'

'Oh!' he perked up, sensing drama.

'He looked furtive, guilty, but he said he was working,' she related, wondering why she was confiding in him. Perhaps it was his sudden interest in conversation. Maybe this could end without rancour after all.

'Well,' he stated, sagely, 'people often say they are working when they are in fact meeting someone, especially hitched folk.' Then flinging his clothes on, as if the chill of their equation had only just reached him, he asked with a fervour that took her aback, 'Did he say what he was working on?' 'A story,' she hazarded, watching his zip go up, marginally missing his greatest asset, 'he's always working on a story.' At which Buff Boy yelped and ran out the door with the same urgency he had shed his clothes earlier, only stopping to say, 'Switch on the TV. You must! Particularly you!'

As the last of the sheets spewed from the printer into their darkened room, his colleague handed them over to Arnie, girding his loins for the test ahead. His spiel to camera being the least of it, he told himself. 'They are waiting,' shouted his partner, her eyes shining with the exhilaration that had infected even her. Arnie started striding down the corridor more scared and excited than he could remember being. Big things were going to happen that day. Life changing things. He could feel it in his bones. As he walked to the cluster of lifts that would take him to the lobby, he was accosted by a man who grabbed him by the lapels. While Arnie spluttered, the no-nonsense fellow miked him up without a single word

exchanged. This could become my life, Arnie thought. He
could learn to like it. Or it could all go pear-shaped.

In the lobby, the camera had already been set up, with a
sensation-hungry crowd seething around it. Arnie walked
the last stretch to it slower than before, scanning his script
for the names he would read out, and considering the
consequences that might befall each. Loss of face, posts,
partners, he was thinking, not without regret, when his
eyes alighted on a name he never thought he would see.
He stumbled and stopped, and didn't know if he could go
on. He could have sworn it wasn't there when he'd looked
earlier. Of course, it wouldn't be, he had said to himself
then, hugely relieved. Things sometimes happened
that weren't meant to. Those little missteps couldn't be
counted, could they? His hesitation was noticed and the
TV director urged him on. 'The whole world is waiting,'
the latter smiled encouragingly.

Arnie pushed on, though his limbs felt as much of
a tangle as his mind. His hand gripping the drastically
cut-down Cheat Sheet he would read on TV trembled so
badly, he worried everyone could see. I won't read this
out, he thought, not this name I can't, and then, with a
spurt of adrenaline, oh, but I must! Vacillating between
'nothing could be worse' and 'this is the best thing to have
happened', he told himself to man up, come clean, start
again. All in Prannoy's voice of course. Then, stepping into
the circle of light awaiting him, he looked heavenwards.
Was she still somewhere on the floors above? Would she
be watching as he wrecked many a megalomaniac? And

their own marriage? Would she understand why he felt compelled to do it? He crossed his fingers tightly behind his back, like she'd taught him to many years ago.

The director counted down and the cameras came alive, hungrily bearing down on him, desperate for the next sensational story. The anchor introduced him from very far away, and he felt disconnected from it all, from this moment of glory he'd lived for and worked towards for years. He bared his teeth for the cameras then and began to tell his story. A story that would shake the world, the anchor had said in introduction, but it was Arnie shaking as he ploughed on. This, he stated, was the story of a rash of websites which helped people cheat on their partners. And hundreds of the world's most sanctimonious political and religious leaders, many of whom had built their careers on their staunch family values, were on them. He talked of the breach of faith involved, not only with partners but with the voting public. Then, he mentioned the thousands whose names he would not be reading out that day. Names he felt no need to read. Every name would become public soon enough, and he left it up to each to deal with it their own way. Fear of being found out would nudge most into action; leave bad relationships, perhaps, or come clean in good ones and start again.

Which was precisely why he had decided to read out one name. Only one everyday name. He fumbled with his papers for the first time since he'd started. The anchor's face, on the monitor next to him, dimmed. The director, from somewhere behind the battalion of blinding lights, whispered encouragement. Arnie collected himself, ready to drop multiple bombs, ending with the one that mattered to him most, when he saw his female colleague at the edge of the circle. She looked on edge too, and he wasn't surprised. But then he noticed their third wheel in the crowd. The third member of his team he had said sayonara to earlier in the day and completely forgotten about. The one who had assured him he would drag a juicy story home. And a sting 'victim' through the mud. But the last they'd heard of him was when he was bawling down the phone about his patsy having flown the coop. Here he was now though, excitedly waving a piece of paper from the front of the crowd. Proffering, it appeared, the contents of a torn page to him.

Startled by Buff Boy's vehemence, Rani switched on the TV. It was afternoon and time for the news, so she flipped to the show Arnie adored and wanted more than anything to be on, one day. She couldn't stop thinking about their encounter in the lobby. And the dotty conversation with her 'date' that had followed. As she watched with only half an eye, the newsreader finished her introduction to some bit of 'breaking news' that would 'shake their world'. They said that about every story, Rani muttered, whether it was about Kate's baby or Rakhi's boobs. The anchor was chattering about a dedicated reporting team that had been tracking this story for a while. A story that was sensational as well as important, they said. A story about betrayal of all sorts, involving thousands of people. Then up came an image on her TV screen that made Rani's blood run cold.

It was the little gemlike app on her phone, the logo for the site she'd stupidly signed up to. At the centre of the storm was this website, the newscaster intoned, while Rani sank fast into a morass of terror. SD let out a jubilant shriek, 'Now it really will be all over!' But Rani reassured herself – with so many thousands on their rolls, as the anchor said, her name may not come to light at all. Or Arnie, lost in a story in the hotel somewhere, might never find out. It *so* wasn't over.

The newsreader then turned to the screen behind her, to welcome the reporter who had broken the news. A local journalist, she said, with a great future. 'And now, we shall have it from the horse's mouth,' she brayed with glee, and the exhausted, exhilarated reporter finally filled the screen. Rani's tears gushed forth then. Wasn't it always going to be Arnie? When had she ever got away with anything? When all her friends had sweets in class, she was the one who'd got caught with her hands in the jar. But she'd much rather have stood outside class for a humiliating hour than lose the love of her life. Was there even the slightest chance now that he might not find out? SD keeled over laughing. Hope, prompted SA, softly in Rani's ear.

She watched and she did hope. She couldn't tear herself away. It was like they say, your life flashing before your eyes. But the flashing lights were around Arnie on TV. In the media scrum, paps and peeps were pushing ever closer in a tightening circle. He continued his story of the rogue websites that hid a multitude of sinners. Rani cringed as he laughed with the anchor over his 'sheets and sheets of cheats'. She sank deeper and deeper into the hotel room bed and her own misery, as the story of transgressions by the world's best known and most righteous was rolled out. At least I am neither of those, she thought. She watched as he reeled off names and the world exploded in glee. Most just wanted the salacious and the sensational. Others awaited their exposure, disappointment or heartbreak. Everyone knew there were more names, and they wanted more. But all Rani wanted was to go back in time, to undo what had been done, and if that could not be, make it right somehow. He'd told the truth. He had been working all along, while she canoodled with men who hadn't mattered a jot. A mass of shame and self-blame, she noticed suddenly a strangely familiar man dart on to the screen. Now where had she seen him before? He was holding a page out to Arnie that the latter appeared not to want, standing as frozen in the spotlight as his wife in front of the TV.

But finally, Arnie accepted the proffered chit. He looked at it for so long, she heard the clock ticking overhead, and sensed the news crew's impatience. Then, he looked up and into the camera, and she could see his distress, but from the set of his chin, his determination also shone through. In a flash, Rani remembered where she had seen the man with the scrap of paper. Only an hour ago, in her room, and rather too much of him at that. And then she knew what was on that page and why he'd left in such a hurry. She knew too that it really was over for her with Arnie, collapsing with such a violent thud in a heap of tears on the bed, that even her shoulder sprites rushed off in fright. But the world continued to watch as Arnie got ready to read out the last name on his list. Rani cowered. She didn't want to see. She didn't want to hear. But the tears couldn't drown out his voice, nor the pillows hide her shame. Most of all, she didn't think she could bear the anger and disgust on his face that was bound to follow. But all he did was put away the piece of paper that had been pushed on him. Then, gazing directly into the camera, with a look of the profoundest contrition Rani had ever seen, she heard Arnie read out his own name.

ROOM FOR TWO

That summer, I thought it would be a good idea to get away from it all.

The Christmas before, Maya had given us a terrible scare by falling so dreadfully ill that we had to rush her to hospital. She was there much longer than expected and required constant care, so I gave up my job to be with her till I was finally allowed to bring her home. The months of anxiety had affected Rohan badly, and he moved out soon after. What I could not understand or explain to his daughter was why he never came back to see her, though I heard from a common acquaintance that he was living with someone nearby.

All in all, it was a very difficult period in our lives, and in the summer, I decided that a holiday was in order.

We packed two small suitcases with just the essentials – clothing, toiletries and a few of Maya's favourite toys and books – and, that afternoon, flew to sun-drenched Corfu, leaving a grey and gloomy England behind us.

Maya was excited. She had been subdued since her illness and her father's inexplicable desertion, but once in the air, her wan face lit up and she spent the whole flight pointing to the Lilliputian landscapes and funny-shaped clouds she saw from the window. The middle-aged man next to me looked irritated, but Maya was enjoying herself after such a long time that I wasn't about to stop her.

I had gone all out to make this a holiday to remember, renting a villa in a lovely lemon grove, despite our constrained circumstances. I couldn't stretch to a pool, but I hoped she would make friends with kids from neighbouring villas quickly and join them at theirs, leaving me time to write. I had just begun freelancing after months off work and it would have to be a working holiday.

We drove past white sand beaches and up winding, wooded roads in our rented car till we reached our villa atop a hill. Maya chattered all the way there as if a stopper had been removed and all the thoughts she'd bottled up inside for so long were pouring out.

'Oh Mommy, look, a freckle (or 'fweckil' as she called it)! The sun's given me my first freckle after aaages!' I looked at the tip of her nose to which she was pointing proudly, but could see nothing. Not wanting to disappoint, however, I laughed and happily agreed.

The sun *was* scorching and the sea shimmered in the heat, but as we drove into the ancient orchards that cocooned our group of villas, the trees shut out the blaze, bathing everything in a green light. It was not what I had expected, but it looked restful, and I could see it being just the thing for us after the trials and tribulations of the past months.

At the end of the road, there was a sign directing us up a narrow overgrown track. The path we jolted over seemed never-ending, but to our delight, we caught glimpses of movement in the undergrowth, which could only have been local fauna. Maya was excited, straining in her seat, eager to get acquainted with her new, but temporary (I made a mental note to rein her enthusiasm in a tad) home. 'Did you see him, Mommy?' 'No,' I said, slightly flustered, 'trying to concentrate on this bendy road, Maya.' And then, with a smile, 'You be my eyes, honey. You always see things I can't.'

Her obvious pleasure in everything justified my decision to spend the summer away from my parents' claustrophobic concern and her father's indifference. My parents were constantly after me to 'let go' and 'move on'; I never understood why, because I neither wanted nor expected Rohan to come back to us. I knew that when we returned, glowing with health and full of our adventures, they would have to accept that we were happy. On our own.

The villa looked very old, older than in the photograph I'd seen, but it had charm. As I heaved open the heavy front door, I could hear the scurry of little feet; not rats I hoped. The sitting room was cool and dark, with even the light streaming in through the patio doors; an undersea-green. Its old-fashioned furniture looked comfortable, if dusty. A tiled corridor led off it, first to a large kitchen

with an imposing old stove and fortunately, tucked away
in a corner, a more modern cooker, belying the villa's
forgotten-for-centuries air. Depositing our luggage in
the first bedroom we came to, we went to have a look
around the rest. The next one along was smaller and
darker, obviously the second bedroom of the brochure. We
wouldn't need two anyway, as Maya had slept in my room
since her ordeal. Then, at the end of the gloomy corridor,
we found an extra door; a room we didn't know we had!
The door to this last room appeared stuck at first, and took
our combined weight (mostly mine, Maya was a wisp of a
thing) to open. It was another small, dark space with twin
beds, but it felt more welcoming somehow, and though
farthest from the sitting area where I planned to work, it
seemed the most suitable playroom for Maya. She took to
it immediately.

'This will be our room, Mommy!' she trilled, slipping
in and out of its shadows impishly, while I scrambled up
to the window, set higher than in any other room, to look
outside. The underbrush was overgrown on this side of
the property, but not unpleasantly, rippling with the life
I'd noticed driving up to the villa. 'Not mine, my love,' I
beamed, 'just yours. A room of your own again.' 'That's
what I said, Mommy, not yours, *ours.*' Lost for a moment
(as I often was these days) in how pale she'd become after
her hospital sojourn, I never got around to correcting her
rather cute royal 'we'.

We settled into a routine over the next few days. After
breakfast on the patio every morning, we would walk to

the beach, which was a brisk trot down the hill, for a dip in the sea. On returning to the villa, I would start work and Maya would gambol in the garden or the 'playroom' by herself for a few hours. I had hoped she would make friends with the other holidaying children, whose voices carried from nearby villas like a constant murmur in the leaves, often seeming much closer than they could be, but the opportunity hadn't arisen yet. That didn't worry me; Maya was very good at keeping herself entertained with her vibrant imagination.

We regrouped for lunch, spending the rest of the day together as I had promised her, going back to my writing to put the finishing touches to the day's effort only after dinner, whilst Maya spent the last half hour before bedtime in her little haven. Days slid by at this gentle pace and after her initial resistance to getting to know the neighbouring kids, Maya made friends with them. I could hear them rampaging with her through our garden, though they never came into the house. What conversation I could catch struck me as entirely one-sided, with Maya doing all the talking. But that's who she was, I chuckled to myself, as I shifted my attention back to my work.

When we bumped into them at the local market, Maya pretended not to know them and vice versa. Yet, isn't that how kids are at that age – keen to keep parents and pals apart? I was just pleased she'd made any friends at all; she had been lonely in Nottingham, where her companions had curiously melted away and she hadn't shown any interest in getting back with them. So, now I left her to her games with her new cohorts in the dense, comfortingly dark garden, and got on with the scribbling.

She appeared to grow particularly attached to a child called Sunny. The first time I realised she was playing with the kids next door was when I heard her calling his name, followed by a glimpse of a small shape rustling in the leaves farther down the main path; she must have been playing hide and seek with real friends for a change. I was so relieved, I almost cried.

Later that week, she dropped the name in conversation at lunchtime. 'Bring your buddy back to the house with you some time,' I urged. Maya smiled and said she did. I knew she meant she would, and made a note to myself (in my head again) to work with her on her grammar after the holiday.

She was happy and that was the important thing, capering all day with her new companions and keen to get away after dinner to the little bedroom down the hall, to lose herself in what sounded like very boisterous games of imagination. That she seemed to want less and less of my company didn't bother me because I wanted that for her, too; her own circle of friends back in Nottingham. Allowing me to take up a full-time job and maybe pick up the thread of my former life; see old confederates, meet someone new ...

I never really knew at what point the sound of the kids' games receded from our garden into the wilderness beyond. Maya still mentioned Sunny occasionally, though only ever in passing. But she had always been secretive, more than ever these past months, and I didn't mind her tendency to slink into her internal world as long as I could keep an eye on her. That I could no longer see or hear her playing from the sitting room window troubled me. Although even when they sounded far away, as though exploring the untended orchards, if I called for Maya, she would emerge from the gloom of the long corridor as if she'd been in the little room all along.

'I heard you, Mommy.'

'Where were you?' I would ask, simultaneously anxious, annoyed and a wee bit pleased with her precocious independence, as one is with spirited children.

She would shake her head and counter, 'But I can hear you, Mommy. Always.' As if that was all that mattered. She wasn't wrong, but I decided to pay more attention to her comings and goings. Over the next few days, whenever the voices stopped murmuring in the garden, I would walk down the corridor to see if Maya had taken refuge in her room. I was worried she was not getting along with her new friends as well as she had initially. She was, after all, very individual.

There was something about the room, too, that had begun to disturb me. It had an atmosphere. Not eerie, quite the opposite. It felt peopled, and comfortable, though it was quite bare but for the two small beds and a large empty cupboard. It would draw me in and make me want to stay. One day, I went in looking for Maya and stayed for hours, daydreaming about the life we would have once I was earning more and Maya had returned to the school she adored. I hadn't re-admitted her after her illness because she was still so fragile.

The next morning, I was back in the room, feeling like I was visiting a confidante for a chat. Everything about it, from the pleasingly faded colours of the patchwork bedspread on which I plumped myself down, to the sunlight trickling almost hesitantly through the high window, had a lulling effect on me. I felt more at peace than I had for a while. I even caught myself humming the songs I used to sing to Maya many moons ago. It felt like a homecoming. An overwhelmingly emotional homecoming that threatened to tear down the defences I had built up in the preceding months of grappling with my misfortunes. When the tears began to flow at long last, I luxuriated in them. But only briefly. My little girl had no one else to hold it together for her. I would have to be strong. I left the room that day, resolved not to intrude into Maya's space again. Yet, there I was the very next day. Soon, I was taking turns with Maya in using her room, seeking its comfort the minute she was out playing with her friends in the mornings. It would wrap itself reassuringly around me like a mother's womb and I craved my time in it. But I knew the hold it had on us was odd, to say the least.

At the end of that week, the cleaning lady who had come by a couple of times before, arrived with a companion who stood guard as she worked, both darting apprehensive glances at us all the while. I got the distinct impression that they were on edge about something they wanted to discuss with me, but didn't know how to start. One of the women finally plucked up the courage to approach me, 'Going home soon? I can't clean this house any more.' I knew immediately that my growing disquiet about the villa was not misplaced. 'Please tell me why,' I implored the women, turning to coax Maya out of earshot as she was very impressionable. Only to see the pair haring off down the path as if they'd seen a ghost! I looked around uneasily, more perturbed than ever.

All that day and into the next, I cajoled and even scolded Maya into accepting that we needed to return to Nottingham without delay, although another two weeks of holiday remained. I could not put my finger on what it was that was upsetting me. It was the unsettling miasma that clung to the villa in its green gloaming. It was the air about it. Thin air. Nothing really. But I didn't want to stay any longer.

'You were unwell for so long that I can't take a chance. We must go back,' I stated as firmly as I could in the face of her relentless young logic. 'But I am better here, Mommy. And I have friends. *A friend.*'

'I know,' I agreed, my heart breaking for her, 'but there's also something here that isn't right (how weak and unconvincing, I thought, even as I said it). We *have* to leave. Nothing can happen to you. Not again.' Then, softly to myself, 'I do not ever mean to lose you.' Perhaps she heard me because she finally gave in, trotting off to her tiny room to collect her toys. I heard two sets of footsteps coming back and turned around quickly. 'Can Sunny come with us?' Maya asked, looking at her companion. I nodded.

There was nobody there, of course, but I could live with that.

I already did.

ACKNOWLEDGEMENTS

I feel I should start by acknowledging the people, places and situations, not always pleasant but unfailingly entertaining, especially in retrospect, that inspired these stories, fiction though they completely are. I must also thank Australia's Transportation Press and the *Open Road Review* in India for publishing two of these previously, 'Lean on Me' and 'The Problem with Potatoes', thus starting me on the road to this collection. More than that, I want to thank my editors, Rea Mukherjee and Udayan Mitra, whose faith in my fiction fashioned this book. But in the end, it is my family who make it all possible, and for them – my love, always.

ABOUT THE AUTHOR

Shreya Sen-Handley is an author, journalist, illustrator and librettist. After years of writing and filming for international media organisations, *National Geographic*, the *Guardian*, the *Times of India*, MTV and BBC amongst them, she has embarked on a book- and opera-writing adventure, collaborating with the Welsh National Opera on a production that will tour the UK in 2020, and with HarperCollins on a clutch of books, including the award-winning *Memoirs of My Body* published in 2017. She has also illustrated for HarperCollins and Hachette, and taught creative writing for British institutions such as the Universities of Nottingham and Cambridge, even as she strives each day to make her children, human and canine, proud (but that's much harder than the rest)!